O. HENRY'S
COPS AND ROBBERS

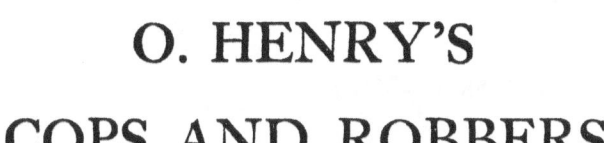

O. Henry's Best Detective and Crime Stories

Fredonia Books
Amsterdam, The Netherlands

Cops and Robbers

by
O. Henry

ISBN: 1-58963-300-8

Copyright © 2001 by Fredonia Books

Reprinted from the 1911 edition

Fredonia Books
Amsterdam, the Netherlands
http://www.fredoniabooks.com

In order to make original editions of historical works
available to scholars at an economical price, this
facsimile of the original edition of 1911 is
reproduced from the best available copy and has
been digitally enhanced to improve legibility, but the
text remains unaltered to retain historical
authenticity.

CONTENTS

COPS...

AND ROBBERS

O. HENRY'S
COPS AND ROBBERS

AFTER TWENTY YEARS

THE policeman on the beat moved up the avenue impressively. The impressiveness was habitual and not for show, for spectators were few. The time was barely 10 o'clock at night, but chilly gusts of wind with a taste of rain in them had well nigh depeopled the streets.

Trying doors as he went, twirling his club with many intricate and artful movements, turning now and then to cast his watchful eye adown the pacific thoroughfare, the officer, with his stalwart form and slight swagger, made a fine picture of a guardian of the peace. The vicinity was one that kept early hours. Now and then you might see the lights of a cigar store or of an all-night lunch counter; but the majority of the doors belonged to business places that had long since been closed.

When about midway of a certain block the policeman suddenly slowed his walk. In the doorway of a darkened hardware store a man leaned, with an unlighted cigar in his mouth. As the policeman walked up to him the man spoke up quickly.

"It's all right, officer," he said, reassuringly. "I'm just waiting for a friend. It's an appointment made twenty years ago. Sounds a little funny to you, doesn't it? Well, I'll explain if you'd like to make certain it's all straight. About that long ago there used to be a restaurant where this store stands — 'Big Joe' Brady's restaurant."

"Until five years ago," said the policeman. "It was torn down then."

The man in the doorway struck a match and lit his cigar. The light showed a pale, square-jawed face with keen eyes, and a little white scar near his right eyebrow. His scarfpin was a large diamond, oddly set.

"Twenty years ago to-night," said the man, "I dined here at 'Big Joe' Brady's with Jimmy Wells, my best chum, and the finest chap in the world. He and I were raised here in New York, just like two brothers, together. I was eighteen and Jimmy was twenty. The next morning I was to start for the West to make my fortune. You couldn't have dragged Jimmy out of New York; he thought it was the only place on earth. Well, we agreed that night that we would meet here again exactly twenty years from that date and time, no matter what our conditions might be or from what distance we might have to come. We figured that in twenty years each of us ought to have our destiny worked out and our fortunes made, whatever they were going to be."

"It sounds pretty interesting," said the policeman. "Rather a long time between meets, though, it seems to me. Haven't you heard from your friend since you left?"

"Well, yes, for a time we corresponded," said the other. "But after a year or two we lost track of each other. You see, the West is a pretty big proposition, and I kept hustling around over it pretty lively. But I know Jimmy will meet me here if he's alive, for he always was the truest, stanchest old chap in the world. He'll never forget. I came a thousand miles to stand in this door to-night, and it's worth it if my old partner turns up."

The waiting man pulled out a handsome watch, the lids of it set with small diamonds.

"Three minutes to ten," he announced. "It was exactly ten o'clock when we parted here at the restaurant door."

"Did pretty well out West, didn't you?" asked the policeman.

"You bet! I hope Jimmy has done half as well. He was a kind of plodder, though, good fellow as he was. I've had to compete with some of the sharpest wits going to get my pile. A man gets in a groove in New York. It takes the West to put a razor-edge on him."

The policeman twirled his club and took a step or two.

"I'll be on my way. Hope your friend comes around all right. Going to call time on him sharp?"

"I should say not!" said the other. "I'll give him half an hour at least. If Jimmy is alive on earth he'll be here by that time. So long, officer."

"Good-night, sir," said the policeman, passing along on his beat, trying doors as he went.

There was now a fine, cold drizzle falling, and the wind had risen from its uncertain puffs into a steady blow. The few foot passengers astir in that quarter hurried dismally and silently along with coat collars turned high and pocketed hands. And in the door of the hardware store the man who had come a thousand miles to fill an appointment, uncertain almost to absurdity, with the friend of his youth, smoked his cigar and waited.

About twenty minutes he waited, and then a tall man in a long overcoat, with collar turned up to his ears, hurried across from the opposite side of the street. He went directly to the waiting man.

"Is that you, Bob?" he asked, doubtfully.

"Is that you, Jimmy Wells?" cried the man in the door.

"Bless my heart!" exclaimed the new arrival, grasping both the other's hands with his own. "It's Bob, sure as fate. I was certain I'd find you here if you were still in existence. Well, well, well! — twenty years is a long time. The old restaurant's gone, Bob; I wish it had lasted, so we could have had another dinner there. How has the West treated you, old man?"

"Bully; it has given me everything I asked it for. You've changed lots, Jimmy. I never thought you were so tall by two or three inches."

"Oh, I grew a bit after I was twenty."

"Doing well in New York, Jimmy?"

"Moderately. I have a position in one of the city departments. Come on, Bob; we'll go around to a place I know of, and have a good long talk about old times."

The two men started up the street, arm in arm. The man from the West, his egotism enlarged by success, was beginning to outline the history of his career. The other, submerged in his overcoat, listened with interest.

At the corner stood a drug store, brilliant with electric lights. When they came into this glare each of them turned simultaneously to gaze upon the other's face.

The man from the West stopped suddenly and released his arm.

"You're not Jimmy Wells," he snapped. "Twenty years is a long time, but not long enough to change a man's nose from a Roman to a pug."

"It sometimes changes a good man into a bad one," said the tall man. "You've been under arrest for ten minutes, 'Silky' Bob. Chicago thinks you may have dropped over our way and wires us she wants to have a chat with you. Going quietly, are you? That's sensible. Now, before we go to the station here's a note I was asked to hand you. You may read it here at the window. It's from Patrolman Wells."

The man from the West unfolded the little piece of paper handed him. His hand was steady when he began to read, but it trembled a little by the time he had finished. The note was rather short.

Bob: I was at the appointed place on time. When you struck the match to light your cigar I saw it was the face of the man wanted in Chicago. Somehow I couldn't do it myself, so I went around and got a plain clothes man to do the job.

                                                                    Jimmy.

THE CLARION CALL

HALF of this story can be found in the records of the Police Department; the other half belongs behind the business counter of a newspaper office.

One afternoon two weeks after Millionaire Norcross was found in his apartment murdered by a burglar, the murderer, while strolling serenely down Broadway, ran plump against Detective Barney Woods.

"Is that you, Johnny Kernan?" asked Woods, who had been near-sighted in public for five years.

"No less," cried Kernan, heartily. "If it isn't Barney Woods, late and early of old Saint Jo! You'll have to show me! What are you doing East? Do the green-goods circulars get out that far?"

"I've been in New York some years," said Woods. "I'm on the city detective force."

"Well, well!" said Kernan, breathing smiling joy and patting the detective's arm.

"Come into Muller's," said Woods, "and let's hunt a quiet table. I'd like to talk to you awhile."

It lacked a few minutes to the hour of four. The tides of trade were not yet loosed, and they found a quiet corner of the café. Kernan, well dressed, slightly swaggering, self-confident, seated himself opposite the little detective, with his pale, sandy mustache, squinting eyes, and ready-made cheviot suit.

"What business are you in now?" asked Woods. "You know you left Saint Jo a year before I did."

"I'm selling shares in a copper mine," said Kernan. "I may establish an office here. Well, well! and so old Barney is a New York detective. You always had a turn that way. You were on the police in Saint Jo after I left there, weren't you?"

"Six months," said Woods. "And now there's one more question, Johnny. I've followed your record pretty close ever since you did that hotel job in Saratoga, and I never knew you to use your gun before. Why did you kill Norcross?"

Kernan stared for a few moments with concentrated attention at the slice of lemon in his high-ball; and then he looked at the detective with a sudden crooked, brilliant smile.

"How did you guess it, Barney?" he asked, admiringly. "I swear I

11

thought the job was as clean and as smooth as a peeled onion. Did I leave a string hanging out anywhere?"

Woods laid upon the table a small gold pencil intended for a watch-charm.

"It's the one I gave you the last Christmas we were in Saint Jo. I've got your shaving mug yet. I found this under a corner of the rug in Norcross's room. I warn you to be careful what you say. I've got it put on to you, Johnny. We were old friends once, but I must do my duty. You'll have to go to the chair for Norcross."

Kernan laughed.

"My luck stays with me," said he. "Who'd have thought old Barney was on my trail!" He slipped one hand inside his coat. In an instant Woods had a revolver against his side.

"Put it away," said Kernan, wrinkling his nose. "I'm only investigating. Aha! It takes nine tailors to make a man, but one can do a man up. There's a hole in that vest pocket. I took that pencil off my chain and slipped it in there in case of a scrap. Put up your gun, Barney, and I'll tell you why I had to shoot Norcross. The old fool started down the hall after me, popping at the buttons on the back of my coat with a peevish little .22 and I had to stop him. The old lady was a darling. She just lay in bed and saw her $12,000 diamond necklace go without a chirp, while she begged like a panhandler to have back a little thin gold ring with a garnet worth about $3. I guess she married old Norcross for his money, all right. Don't they hang on to the little trinkets from the, Man Who Lost Out, though? There were six rings, two brooches and a chatelaine watch. Fifteen thousand would cover the lot."

"I warned you not to talk," said Woods.

"Oh, that's all right," said Kernan. "The stuff is in my suit case at the hotel. And now I'll tell you why I'm talking. Because it's safe. I'm talking to a man I know. You owe me a thousand dollars, Barney Woods, and even if you wanted to arrest me your hand wouldn't make the move."

"I haven't forgotten," said Woods. "You counted out twenty fifties without a word. I'll pay it back some day. That thousand saved me and — well, they were piling my furniture out on the sidewalk when I got back to the house."

"And so," continued Kernan, "you being Barney Woods, born as true as steel, and bound to play the game, can't lift one little finger to arrest the man you're indebted to. Oh, I have to study men as well as Yale locks and window fastenings in my business. Now, keep quiet while I ring for the waiter. I've had a thirst for a year or two that worries me a little. If I'm ever caught the lucky sleuth will have to divide honors with the old boy Booze. But I never drink during business hours. After a job I can crook elbows with my old friend Barney with a clear conscience. What are you taking?"

The waiter came with the little decanters and the siphon and left them alone again.

"You've called the turn," said Woods, as he rolled the little gold pencil about with a thoughtful forefinger. "I've got to pass you up. I can't lay a hand on you. If I'd a-paid that money back — but I didn't, and that settles it. It's a bad break I'm making, Johnny, but I can't dodge it. You helped me once, and it calls for the same."

"I knew it," said Kernan, raising his glass, with a flushed smile of self-appreciation. "I can judge men. Here's to Barney, for — 'he's a jolly good fellow.' "

"I don't believe," went on Woods quietly, as if he were thinking aloud, "that if accounts had been square between you and me, all the money in all the banks in New York could have bought you out of my hands tonight."

"I know it couldn't," said Kernan. "That's why I knew I was safe with you."

"Most people," continued the detective, "look sideways at my business. They don't class it among the fine arts and the professions. But I've always taken a kind of fool pride in it. And here is where I go 'busted.' I guess I'm a man first and a detective afterward. I've got to let you go, and then I've got to resign from the force. I guess I can drive an express wagon. Your thousand dollars is further off than ever."

"Oh, you're welcome to it," said Kernan, with a lordly air. "I'd be willing to call the debt off, but I know you wouldn't have it. It was a lucky day for me when you borrowed it. And now, let's drop the subject. I'm off to the West on a morning train. I know a place out there where I can negotiate the Norcross sparks. Drink up, Barney, and forget your troubles. We'll have a jolly time while the police are knocking their heads together over the case. I've got one of my Sahara thirsts on to-night. But I'm in the hands — the unofficial hands — of my old friend Barney, and I won't even dream of a cop."

And then, as Kernan's ready finger kept the button and the waiter working, his weak point — a tremendous vanity and arrogant egotism, began to show itself. He recounted story after story of his successful plunderings, ingenious plots and infamous transgressions until Woods, with all his familiarity with evil-doers, felt growing within him a cold abhorrence toward the utterly vicious man who had once been his benefactor.

"I'm disposed of, of course," said Woods, at length. "But I advise you to keep under cover for a spell. The newspapers may take up this Norcross affair. There has been an epidemic of burglaries and manslaughter in town this summer."

The word sent Kernan into a high glow of sullen, vindictive rage.

"To h — l with the newspapers," he growled. "What do they spell but brag and blow and boodle in box-car letters? Suppose they do take up a case — what does it amount to? The police are easy enough to fool; but what do the newspapers do? They send a lot of pin-head reporters around to the scene; and they make for the nearest saloon and have beer while they take photos of the bartender's oldest daughter in evening dress to print as the fiancée of the young man in the tenth story, who thought he heard a noise below on the night of the murder. That's about as near as the newspapers ever come to running down Mr. Burglar."

"Well, I don't know," said Woods, reflecting. "Some of the papers have done good work in that line. There's the *Morning Mars,* for instance. It warmed up two or three trails, and got the man after the police had let 'em get cold."

"I'll show you," said Kernan, rising, and expanding his chest. "I'll show you what I think of newspapers in general, and your *Morning Mars* in particular."

Three feet from their table was the telephone booth. Kernan went inside and sat at the instrument, leaving the door open. He found a number in the book, took down the receiver and made his demand upon Central. Woods sat still, looking at the sneering, cold, vigilant face waiting close to the transmitter, and listened to the words that came from the thin, truculent lips curved into a contemptuous smile.

"That the *Morning Mars?* . . . I want to speak to the managing editor. . . . Why, tell him it's someone who wants to talk to him about the Norcross murder.

"You the editor? . . . All right. . . . I am the man who killed old Norcross. . . . Wait! Hold the wire; I'm not the usual crank . . . Oh, there isn't the slightest danger. I've just been discussing it with a detective friend of mine. I killed the old man at 2.30 A.M. two weeks ago tomorrow. . . . Have a drink with you? Now, hadn't you better leave that kind of talk to your funny man? Can't you tell whether a man's guying you or whether you're being offered the biggest scoop your dull dishrag of a paper ever had? . . . Well, that's so; it's a bobtail scoop — but you can hardly expect me to 'phone in my name and address. . . . Why! Oh, because I heard you make a specialty of solving mysterious crimes that stump the police. . . . No, that's not all. I want to tell you that your rotten, lying penny sheet is of no more use in tracking an intelligent murderer or highway man than a blind poodle would be. . . . What? . . . Oh, no, this isn't a rival newspaper office; you're getting it straight. I did the Norcross job, and I've got the jewels in my suit case at — 'the name of the hotel could not be learned' — you recognize that phrase, don't you? I thought so. You've used it often enough. Kind of rattles you, doesn't it, to have the mysterious villain call up your great, big, all-powerful organ of right and justice and good government and tell you what a helpless old gas-bag you are? . . . Cut that out; you're not that big a fool — no, you don't think I'm a fraud. I can tell it by your voice. . . . Now, listen, and I'll give you a pointer that will prove it to you. Of course you've had this murder case worked over by your staff of bright young blockheads. Half of the second button on old Mrs. Norcross's nightgown is broken off. I saw it when I took the garnet ring off her finger. I thought it was a ruby. . . . Stop that! It won't work."

Kernan turned to Woods with a diabolic smile.

"I've got him going. He believes me now. He didn't quite cover the transmitter with his hand when he told somebody to call up Central on another 'phone and get our number. I'll give him just one more dig and then we'll make a 'get-away.'

"Hello! . . . Yes. I'm here yet. You didn't think I'd run from such a little subsidized, turncoat rag of a newspaper, did you? . . . Have me inside of forty-eight hours? Say, will you quit being funny? Now, you let grown men alone and attend to your business of hunting up divorce cases and street-car accidents and printing the filth and scandal that you make your living by. Good-by, old boy — sorry I haven't time to call on you. I'd feel perfectly safe in your sanctum asinorum. Tra-la!

"He's as mad as a cat that's lost a mouse," said Kernan, hanging up the receiver and coming out. "And now, Barney, my old boy, we'll go to a show and enjoy ourselves until a reasonable bedtime. Four hours' sleep for me, and then the west-bound."

The two dined in a Broadway restaurant. Kernan was pleased with himself. He spent money like a prince of fiction. And then a weird and gorgeous musical comedy engaged their attention. Afterward there was a late supper in a grill-room, with champagne, and Kernan at the height of his complacency.

Half-past three in the morning found them in a corner of an all-night café, Kernan still boasting in a vapid and rambling way, Woods thinking moodily over the end that had come to his usefulness as an upholder of the law. But, as he pondered, his eye brightened with a speculative light. "I wonder if it's possible," he said to himself, "I won-der if it's pos-si-ble!"

And then outside the café the comparative stillness of the early morning was punctured by faint, uncertain cries that seemed mere fireflies of sound, some growing louder, some fainter, waxing and waning amid the rumble of milk wagons and infrequent cars. Shrill cries they were when near — well-known cries that conveyed many meanings to the ears of those of the slumbering millions of the great city who waked to hear them. Cries that bore upon their significant, small volume the weight of a world's woe and laughter and delight and stress. To some, cowering beneath the protection of a night's ephemeral cover, they brought news of the hideous, bright day; to others, wrapped in happy sleep, they announced a morning that would dawn blacker than sable night. To many of the rich they brought a besom to sweep away what had been theirs while the stars shone; to the poor they brought — another day.

All over the city the cries were starting up, keen and sonorous, heralding the chances that the slipping of one cogwheel in the machinery of time had made; apportioning to the sleepers while they lay at the mercy of fate, the vengeance, profit, grief, reward and doom that the new figure in the calendar had brought them. Shrill and yet plaintive were the cries, as if the young voices grieved that so much evil and so little good was in their irresponsible hands. Thus echoed in the streets of the helpless city the transmission of the latest decrees of the gods, the cries of the newsboys — the Clarion Call of the Press.

Woods flipped a dime to the waiter, and said:

"Get me a *Morning Mars*."

When the paper came he glanced at its first page, and then tore a leaf out of his memorandum book and began to write on it with the little gold pencil. "What's the news?" yawned Kernan.

Woods flipped over to him the piece of writing:

The New York *Morning Mars:*

Please pay to the order of John Kernan the one thousand dollars reward coming to me for his arrest and conviction.

                                        BARNARD WOODS.

"I kind of thought they would do that," said Woods, "when you were jollying 'em so hard. Now, Johnny, you'll come to the police station with me."

A MUNICIPAL REPORT

The cities are full of pride,
    Challenging each to each—
This from her mountainside,
This from her mountainside,

R. KIPLING.

Fancy a novel about Chicago or Buffalo, let us say, or of Nashville, Tennessee! There are just three big cities in the United States that are "story cities" — New York, of course, New Orleans, and, best of the lot, San Francisco. —

FRANK NORRIS.

EAST is East, and West is San Francisco, according to Californians. Californians are a race of people; they are not merely inhabitants of a State. They are the Southerners of the West. Now, Chicagoans are no less loyal to their city; but when you ask them why, they stammer and speak of lake fish and the new Odd Fellows Building. But Californians go into detail.

Of course they have, in the climate, an argument that is good for half an hour while you are thinking of your coal bills and heavy underwear. But as soon as they come to mistake your silence for conviction, madness comes upon them, and they picture the city of the Golden Gate as the Bagdad of the New World. So far, as a matter of opinion, no refutation is necessary. But dear cousins all (from Adam and Eve descended), it is a rash one who will lay his finger on the map and say: "In this town there can be no romance — what could happen here?" Yes, it is a bold and a rash deed to challenge in one sentence history, romance, and Rand and McNally.

NASHVILLE. — A city, port of delivery, and the capital of the State of Tennessee, is on the Cumberland River and on the N. C. & St. L. and the L. & N. railroads. This city is regarded as the most important educational centre in the South.

I stepped off the train at 8 P. M. Having searched the thesaurus in vain for adjectives, I must, as a substitution, hie me to comparison in the form of a recipe.

17

Take of London for 30 parts; malaria 10 parts; gas leaks 20 parts; dewdrops gathered in a brick yard at sunrise, 25 parts; odor of honeysuckle 15 parts. Mix.

The mixture will give you an approximate conception of a Nashville drizzle. It is not so fragrant as a moth-ball nor as thick as pea-soup; but 'tis enough — 'twill serve.

I went to a hotel in a tumbril. It required strong self-suppression for me to keep from climbing to the top of it and giving an imitation of Sidney Carton. The vehicle was drawn by beasts of a bygone era and driven by something dark and emancipated.

I was sleepy and tired, so when I got to the hotel I hurriedly paid it the fifty cents it demanded (with approximate lagniappe, I assure you). I knew its habits; and I did not want to hear it prate about its old "marster" or anything that happened "befo' de wah."

The hotel was one of the kind described as "renovated." That means $20,000 worth of new marble pillars, tiling, electric lights and brass cuspidors in the lobby, and a new L. & N. time table and a lithograph of Lookout Mountain in each one of the great rooms above. The management was beyond reproach, the attention full of exquisite Southern courtesy, the service as slow as the progress of a snail and as good-humored as Rip Van Winkle. The food was worth traveling a thousand miles for. There is no other hotel in the world where you can get such chicken livers *en brochette*.

At dinner I asked a Negro waiter if there was anything doing in town. He pondered gravely for a minute, and then replied: "Well, boss, I don't really reckon there's anything at all doin' after sundown."

Sundown had been accomplished; it had been drowned in the drizzle long before. So that spectacle was denied me. But I went forth upon the streets in the drizzle to see what might be there.

It is built on undulating grounds; and the streets are lighted by electricity at a cost of $32,470 per annum.

As I left the hotel there was a race riot. Down upon me charged a company of freedmen, or Arabs, or Zulus, armed with — no, I saw with relief that they were not rifles, but whips. And I saw dimly a caravan of black, clumsy vehicles; and at the reassuring shouts, "Kyar you anywhere in the town, boss, fuh fifty cents," I reasoned that I was merely a "fare" instead of a victim.

I walked through long streets, all leading uphill. I wondered how those streets ever came down again. Perhaps they didn't until they were "graded." On a few of the "main streets" I saw lights in stores here and there; saw street cars go by conveying worthy burghers hither and yon; saw people pass engaged in the art of conversation, and heard a burst of semi-lively laughter issuing from a soda-water and ice-cream parlor. The streets other than "main" seemed to have enticed upon their borders houses consecrated to peace and domesticity. In many of them lights shone behind discreetly drawn window shades, in a few pianos tinkled orderly and irreproachable music. There was, indeed, little "doing." I wished I had come before sundown. So I returned to my hotel.

In November, 1864, the Confederate General Hood advanced against Nashville, where he shut up a National force under General Thomas. The latter then sallied forth and defeated the Confederates in a terrible conflict.

All my life I have heard of, admired, and witnessed the fine marksmanship of the South in its peaceful conflicts in the tobacco-chewing regions. But in my hotel a surprise awaited me. There were twelve bright, new, imposing, capacious brass cuspidors in the great lobby, tall enough to be called urns and so wide-mouthed that the crack pitcher of a lady baseball team should have been able to throw a ball into one of them at five paces distant. But, although a terrible battle had raged and was still raging, the enemy had not suffered. Bright, new, imposing, capacious, untouched, they stood. But shades of Jefferson Brick! the tile floor — the beautiful tile floor! I could not avoid thinking of the battle of Nashville, and trying to draw, as is my foolish habit, some deductions about hereditary marksmanship.

Here I first saw Major (by misplaced courtesy) Wentworth Caswell. I knew him for a type the moment my eyes suffered from the sight of him. A rat has no geographical habitat. My old friend, A. Tennyson, said, as he so well said almost everything:

> Prophet, curse me the blabbing lip,
> And curse me the British vermin, the rat.

Let us regard the word "British" as interchangeable ad lib. A rat is a rat.

This man was hunting about the hotel lobby like a starved dog that had forgotten where he had buried a bone. He had a face of great acreage, red, pulpy, and with a kind of sleepy massiveness like that of

Buddha. He possessed one single virtue — he was very smoothly shaven. The mark of the beast is not indelible upon a man until he goes about with a stubble. I think that if he had not used his razor that day I would have repulsed his advances, and the criminal calendar of the world would have been spared the addition of one murder.

I happened to be standing within five feet of a cuspidor when Major Caswell opened fire upon it. I had been observant enough to perceive that the attacking force was using Gatlings instead of squirrel rifles, so I sidestepped so promptly that the major seized the opportunity to apologize to a noncombatant. He had the blabbing lip. In four minutes he had become my friend and had dragged me to the bar.

I desire to interpolate here that I am a Southerner. But I am not one by profession or trade. I eschew the string tie, the slouch hat, the Prince Albert, the number of bales of cotton destroyed by Sherman, and plug chewing. When the orchestra plays "Dixie" I do not cheer. I slide a little lower on the leather-cornered seat and, well, order another Würzburger and wish that Longstreet had — but what's the use?

Major Caswell banged the bar with his fist, and the first gun at Fort Sumter reechoed. When he fired the last one at Appomattox I began to hope. But then he began on family trees, and demonstrated that Adam was only a third cousin of a collateral branch of the Caswell family. Genealogy disposed of, he took up, to my distaste, his private family matters. He spoke of his wife, traced her descent back to Eve, and profanely denied any possible rumor that she may have had relations in the land of Nod.

By this time I began to suspect that he was trying to obscure by noise the fact that he had ordered the drinks, on the chance that I would be bewildered into paying for them. But when they were down he crashed a silver dollar loudly upon the bar. Then, of course, another serving was obligatory. And when I had paid for that I took leave of him brusquely; for I wanted no more of him. But before I had obtained my release he had prated loudly of an income that his wife received, and showed a handful of silver money.

When I got my key at the desk the clerk said to me courteously: "If that man Caswell has annoyed you, and if you would like to make a complaint, we will have him ejected. He is a nuisance, a loafer, and without any known means of support, although he seems to have some money most of the time. But we don't seem to be able to hit upon any means of throwing him out legally."

"Why, no," said I, after some reflection; "I don't see my way clear to making a complaint. But I would like to place myself on record as asserting that I do not care for his company. Your town," I continued "seems to be a quiet one. What manner of entertainment, adventure, or excitement have you to offer to the stranger within your gates?"

"Well, sir," said the clerk, "there will be a show here next Thursday. It is — I'll look it up and have the announcement sent up to your room with the ice water. Good-night."

After I went up to my room I looked out the window. It was only about ten o'clock, but I looked upon a silent town. The drizzle continued, spangled with dim lights, as far apart as currants in a cake sold at the Ladies' Exchange.

"A quiet place," I said to myself, as my first shoe struck the ceiling of the occupant of the room beneath mine. "Nothing of the life here that gives color and good variety to the cities in the East and West. Just a good, ordinary, humdrum, business town."

Nashville occupies a foremost place among the manufacturing centres of the country. It is the fifth boot and shoe market in the United States, the largest candy and cracker manufacturing city in the South, and does an enormous wholesale drygoods, grocery, and drug business.

I must tell you how I came to be in Nashville, and I assure you the digression brings as much tedium to me as it does to you. I was traveling elsewhere on my own business, but I had a commission from a Northern literary magazine to stop over there and establish a personal connection between the publication and one of its contributors, Azalea Adair.

Adair (there was no clue to the personality except the handwriting) had sent in some essays (lost art!) and poems that had made the editors swear approvingly over their one o'clock luncheon. So they had commissioned me to round up said Adair and corner by contract his or her output at two cents a word before some other publisher offered her ten or twenty.

At nine o'clock the next morning, after my chicken livers *en brochette* (try them if you can find that hotel), I strayed out into the drizzle, which was still on for an unlimited run. At the first corner I came upon Uncle Cæsar. He was a stalwart Negro, older than the pyramids, with gray wool and a face that reminded me of Brutus, and a second afterwards of the late King Cettiwayo. He wore the most remarkable coat that I ever had seen or expect to see. It reached to his ankles and had once been a Confederate gray in colors. But rain and sun and age had so variegated it that Joseph's coat, beside it, would have faded to a pale monochrome. I must linger with that coat, for it has to do with the story — the story that is so long in coming, because you can hardly expect anything to happen in Nashville.

Once it must have been the military coat of an officer. The cape of it had vanished, but all adown its front it had been frogged and tasseled magnificently. But now the frogs and tassels were gone. In their stead had been patiently stitched (I surmised by some surviving "black mammy") new frogs made of cunningly twisted common hempen twine. This twine was frayed and disheveled. It must have been added to the coat as a substitute for vanished splendors, with tasteless but painstaking devotion, for it followed faithfully the curves of the long-missing frogs. And, to complete the comedy and pathos of the garment, all its buttons were gone save one. The second button from the top alone remained. The coat was fastened by other twine strings tied through the buttonholes and other holes rudely pierced in the opposite side. There was never such a weird garment so fantastically bedecked and of so many mottled hues. The lone button was the size of a half-dollar, made of yellow horn and sewed on with coarse twine.

This Negro stood by a carriage so old that Ham himself might have started a hack line with it after he left the ark with the two animals hitched to it. As I approached he threw open the door, drew out a feather duster, waved it without using it, and said in deep, rumbling tones:

"Step right in, suh; ain't a speck of dust in it — jus' got back from a funeral, suh."

I inferred that on such gala occasions carriages were given an extra cleaning. I looked up and down the street and perceived that there was little choice among the vehicles for hire that lined the curb. I looked in my memorandum book for the address of Azalea Adair.

"I want to go to 861 Jessamine Street," I said, and was about to step into the hack. But for an instant the thick, long, gorilla-like arm of the Negro barred me. On his massive and saturnine face a look of sudden suspicion and enmity flashed for a moment. Then, with quickly returning conviction, he asked, blandishingly; "What are you gwine there for, boss?"

"What is that to you?" I asked, a little sharply.

"Nothin', suh, jus' nothin'. Only it's a lonesome kind of part of town and few folks ever has business out there. Step right in. The seats is clean — jes' got back from a funeral, suh."

A mile and a half it must have been to our journey's end. I could hear nothing but the fearful rattle of the ancient hack over the uneven brick paving; I could smell nothing but the drizzle, now further flavored with coal smoke and something like a mixture of tar and oleander blossoms. All I could see through the streaming windows were two rows of dim houses.

The city has an area of 10 square miles; 181 miles of streets, of which 137 miles are paved; a system of waterworks that cost $2,000,000, with 77 miles of mains.

Eight-sixty-one Jessamine Street was a decayed mansion. Thirty yards back from the street it stood, outmerged in a splendid grove of trees and untrimmed shrubbery. A row of box bushes overflowed and almost hid the paling fence from sight; the gate was kept closed by a rope noose that encircled the gate post and the first paling of the gate. But when you got inside you saw that 861 was a shell, a shadow, a ghost of former grandeur and excellence. But in the story, I have not yet got inside.

When the hack had ceased from rattling and the weary quadrupeds came to a rest I handed my jehu his fifty cents with an additional quarter, feeling a glow of conscious generosity as I did so. He refused it.

"It's two dollars, suh," he said.

"How's that?" I asked. "I plainly heard you call out at the hotel. 'Fifty cents to any part of the town.'"

"It's two dollars, suh," he repeated obstinately. "It's a long ways from the hotel."

"It is within the city limits and well within them," I argued. "Don't think that you have picked up a greenhorn Yankee. Do you see those hills over there?" I went on, pointing toward the east (I could not see them, myself, for the drizzle); "well, I was born and raised on their other side. You old fool, can't you tell people from other people when you see 'em?"

The grim face of King Cettiwayo softened. "Is you from the South, suh? I reckon it was them shoes of yourn fooled me. They is somethin' sharp in the toes for a Southern gen'l'man to wear."

"Then the charge is fifty cents, I suppose?" said I, inexorably.

His former expression, a mingling of cupidity and hostility, returned, remained ten seconds, and vanished.

"Boss," he said, "fifty cents is right; but I *needs* two dollars, suh;

I'm *obleeged* to have two dollars. I ain't *demandin'* it now, suh; after I knows whar you's from; I'm jus' sayin' that I *has* to have two dollars to-night and business is mighty po'."

Peace and, confidence settled upon his heavy features. He had been luckier than he had hoped. Instead of having picked up a greenhorn, ignorant of rates, he had come upon an inheritance.

"You confounded old rascal," I said, reaching down to my pocket, "you ought to be turned over to the police."

For the first time I saw him smile. He knew; *he knew;* HE KNEW.

I gave him two one dollar bills. As I handed them over I noticed that one of them had seen parlous times. It's upper right-hand corner was missing, and it had been torn through the middle, but joined again. A strip of blue tissue paper, pasted over the split, preserved its negotiability.

Enough of the African bandit for the present: I'left him happy, lifted the rope, and opened the creaky gate.

The house, as I said, was a shell. A paint brush had not touched it in twenty years. I could not see why a strong wind should not have bowled it over like a house of cards until I looked again at the trees that hugged it close — the trees that saw the battle of Nashville and still drew their protecting branches around it against storm and enemy and cold.

Azalea Adair, fifty years old, white-haired, a descendant of the cavaliers, as thin and frail as the house she lived in, robed in the cheapest and cleanest dress I ever saw, with an air as simple as a queen's, received me.

The reception room seemed a mile square, because there was nothing in it except some rows of books, on unpainted white-pine bookshelves, a cracked marble-topped, table, a rag rug, a hairless horsehair sofa, and two or three chairs. Yes, there was a picture on the wall, a colored crayon drawing of a cluster of pansies. I looked around for the portrait of Andrew Jackson and the pinecone hanging basket but they were not there.

Azalea Adair and I had conversation, a little of which will be repeated to you. She was a product of the old South, gently nurtured in the sheltered life. Her learning was not broad, but was deep and of splendid originality in its somewhat narrow scope. She had been educated at home, and her knowledge of the world was derived from inference and by inspiration. Of such is the precious, small group of essayists made. While she talked to me I kept brushing my fingers, trying, unconsciously, to rid them guiltily of the absent dust from the half-calf backs of Lamb, Chaucer, Hazlitt, Marcus Aurelius, Montaigne, and Hood. She was exquisite, she was a valuable discovery. Nearly everybody nowadays knows too much — oh, so much too much — of real life.

I could perceive clearly that Azalea Adair was very poor. A house and a dress she had, not much else, I fancied. So, divided between my duty to the magazine and my loyalty to the poets and essayists who fought Thomas in the valley of the Cumberland, I listened to her voice which was like a harpsichord's, and found that I could not speak of contracts. In the presence of the nine Muses and the three Graces one hesitated to lower the topic to two cents. There would have to be another colloquy after I had regained my commercialism. But I spoke of my mission, and three o'clock of the next afternoon was set for the discussion of the business proposition.

"Your town," I said, as I began to make ready to depart (which is the time for smooth generalities) "seems to be a quiet, sedate place. A home town, I should say, where few things out of the ordinary ever happen."

It carries on an extensive trade in stoves and hollow ware with the West and South, and its flourishing mills have a daily capacity of more than 2,000 barrels.

Azalea Adair seemed to reflect.

"I have never thought of it that way," she said, with a kind of sincere intensity that seemed to belong to her. "Isn't it in the still, quiet places that things do happen? I fancy that when God began to create the earth on the first Monday morning one could have leaned out one's window and heard the drops of mud splashing from His trowel as He built up the everlasting hills. What did the noisiest project in the world — I mean the building of the tower of Babel — result in finally? A page and a half of Esperanto in the *North American Review*."

"Of course," said I, platitudinously, "human nature is the same everywhere; but there is more color — er — more drama and movement and — er — romance in some cities than in others."

"On the surface," said Azalea Adair. "I have traveled many times around the world in a golden airship wafted on two wings — print and dreams. I have seen (on one of my imaginary tours) the Sultan of Turkey bowstring with his own hands one of his wives who had uncovered her face in public. I have seen a man in Nashville tear up his theatre tickets because his wife was going out with her face covered — with rice powder. In San Francisco's Chinatown I saw the slave girl

Sing Yee dipped slowly, inch by inch, in boiling almond oil to make her swear she would never see her American lover again. She gave in when the boiling oil had reached three inches above her knee. At a euchre party in East Nashville the other night I saw Kitty Morgan cut dead by seven of her schoolmates and lifelong friends because she had married a house painter. The boiling oil was sizzling as high as her heart; but I wish you could have seen the fine little smile that she carried from table to table. Oh, yes, it is a humdrum town. Just a few miles of red brick houses and mud and stores and lumber yards."

Some one had knocked hollowly at the back of the house. Azalea Adair breathed a soft apology and went to investigate the sound. She came back in three minutes with brightened eyes, a faint flush on her cheeks, and ten years lifted from her shoulders.

"You must have a cup of tea before you go," she said "and a sugar cake."

She reached and shook a little iron bell. In shuffled a small Negro girl about twelve, barefoot, not very tidy, glowering at me with thumb in mouth and bulging eyes.

Azalea Adair opened a tiny, worn purse and drew out a dollar bill, a dollar bill with the upper right-hand corner missing, torn in two pieces and pasted together again with a strip of blue tissue paper. It was one of those bills I had given the piratical Negro — there was no doubt of it.

"Go up to Mr. Baker's store on the corner, Impy," she said, handing the girl the dollar bill, "and get a quarter of a pound of tea — the kind he always sends me — and ten cents' worth of sugar cakes. Now, hurry. The supply of tea in the house happens to be exhausted," she explained to me.

Impy left by the back way. Before the scrape of her hard, bare feet had died away on the back porch, a wild shriek — I was sure it was hers — filled the hollow house. Then the deep, gruff tones of an angry man's voice mingled with the girl's further squeals and unintelligible words.

Azalea Adair rose without surprise or emotion and disappeared. For two minutes I heard the hoarse rumble of the man's voice; then something like an oath and a slight scuffle, and she returned calmly to her chair.

"This is a roomy house," she said, "and I have a tenant for part of it. I am sorry to have to rescind my invitation to tea. It is impossible to get the kind I always use at the store. Perhaps to-morrow Mr. Baker will be able to supply me."

I was sure that Impy had not had time to leave the house. I inquired concerning street-car lines and took my leave. After I was well on my way I remembered that I had not learned Azalea Adair's name. But to-morrow would do.

That same day I started in on the course of iniquity that this uneventful city forced upon me. I was in the town only two days, but in that time I managed to lie shamelessly by telegraph, and to be an accomplice — after the fact, if that is the correct legal term — to a murder.

As I rounded the corner nearest my hotel the Afrite coachman of the polychromatic, nonpareil coat seized me, swung open the dungeony door of his peripatetic sarcophagus, flirted his feather duster and began his ritual: "Step right in, boss. Carriage is clean — jus' got back from a funeral. Fifty cents to any ——"

And then he knew me and grinned broadly. " 'Scuse me, boss; you is de gen'l'man what rid out with me dis mawnin'. Thank you kindly, suh."

"I am going out to 861 again to-morrow afternoon at three," said I, "and if you will be here, I'll let you drive me. So you know Miss Adair?" I concluded, thinking of my dollar bill.

"I belonged to her father, Judge Adair, suh," he replied.

"I judge that she is pretty poor," I said. "She hasn't much money to speak of, has she?"

For an instant I looked again at the fierce countenance of King Cettiwayo, and then he changed back to an extortionate old Negro hack driver.

"She ain't gwine to starve, suh," he answered, slowly. "She has reso'ces, suh; she has reso'ces."

"I shall pay you fifty cents for the trip," said I.

"Dat is puffeckly correct, suh," he answered, humbly. "I jus' had to have dat two dollars dis mawnin', boss."

I went to the hotel and lied by electricity. I wired the magazine: "A. Adair holds out for eight cents a word."

The answer that came back was: "Give it to her quick, you duffer."

Just before dinner "Major" Wentworth Caswell bore down upon me with the greetings of a long-lost friend. I have seen few men whom I have so instantaneously hated, and of whom it was so difficult to be rid. I was standing at the bar when he invaded me; therefore I could not wave the white ribbon in his face. I would have paid gladly for the drinks, hoping thereby, to escape another; but he was one of those despicable, roaring, advertising bibbers who must have brass bands and fireworks attend upon every cent that they waste on their follies.

With an air of producing millions he drew two one-dollar bills from a pocket and dashed one of them upon the bar. I looked once more at the dollar bill with the upper right-hand corner missing, torn through the middle, and patched with a strip of blue tissue paper. It was my dollar bill again. It could have been no other.

I went up to my room. The drizzle and the monotony of a dreary, eventless Southern town had made me tired and listless. I remember that just before I went to bed I mentally disposed of the mysterious dollar bill (which might have formed the clue to a tremendously fine detective story of San Francisco) by saying to myself sleepily: "Seems as if a lot of people here own stock in the Hack-Driver's Trust. Pays dividends promptly, too. Wonder if ——" Then I fell asleep.

King Cettiwayo was at his post the next day, and rattled my bones over the stones out to 861. He was to wait and rattle me back again when I was ready.

Azalea Adair looked paler and cleaner and frailer than she had looked on the day before. After she had signed the contract at eight cents per word she grew still paler and began to slip out of her chair. Without much trouble I managed to get her up on the antediluvian horsehair sofa and then I ran out to the sidewalk and yelled to the coffee-colored Pirate to bring a doctor. With a wisdom that I had not suspected in him, he abandoned his team and struck off up the street afoot, realizing the value of speed. In ten minutes he returned with a grave, gray-haired, and capable man of medicine. In a few words (worth much less than eight cents each) I explained to him my presence in the hollow house of mystery. He bowed with stately understanding, and turned to the old Negro.

"Uncle Cæsar," he said, calmly, "run up to my house and ask Miss Lucy to give you a cream pitcher full of fresh milk and half a tumbler of port wine. And hurry back. Don't drive — run. I want you to get back sometime this week."

It occurred to me that Dr. Merriman also felt a distrust as to the speeding powers of the land-pirate's steeds. After Uncle Cæsar was gone, lumberingly, but swiftly, up the street, the doctor looked me over with great politeness and as much careful calculation until he decided that I might do.

"It is only a case of insufficient nutrition," he said. "In other words, the result of poverty, pride, and starvation. Mrs. Caswell has many devoted friends who would be glad to aid her, but she will accept nothing except from that old Negro, Uncle Cæsar, who was once owned by her family."

"Mrs. Caswell!" said I, in surprise. And then I looked at the contract and saw that she had signed it "Azalea Adair Caswell."

"I thought she was Miss Adair," I said.

"Married to a drunken, worthless loafer, sir," said the doctor. "It is said that he robs her even of the small sums that her old servant contributes toward her support."

When the milk and wine had been brought the doctor soon revived Azalea Adair. She sat up and talked of the beauty of the autumn leaves that were then in season and their height of color. She referred lightly to her fainting seizure as the outcome of an old palpitation of the heart. Impy fanned her as she lay on the sofa. The doctor was due elsewhere, and I followed him to the door. I told him that it was within my power and intentions to make a reasonable advance of money to Azalea Adair on future contributions to the magazine, and he seemed pleased.

"By the way," he said, "perhaps you would like to know that you have had royalty for a coachman. Old Cæsar's grandfather was a king in Congo. Cæsar himself has royal ways, as you may have observed."

As the doctor was moving off I heard Uncle Cæsar's voice inside: "Did he git bofe of dem two dollars from you, Mis' Zalea?"

"Yes, Cæsar," I heard Azalea Adair answer, weakly. And then I went in and concluded business negotiations with our contributor. I assumed the responsibility of advancing fifty dollars, putting it as a necessary formality in binding our bargain. And then Uncle Cæsar drove me back to the hotel.

Here ends all of the story as far as I can testify as a witness. The rest must be only bare statements of facts.

At about six o'clock I went out for a stroll. Uncle Cæsar was at his corner. He threw open the door of his carriage, flourished his duster, and began his depressing formula: "Step right in, suh. Fifty cents to anywhere in the city — hack's puffickly clean, suh — jus' got back from a funeral ——"

And then he recognized me. I think his eyesight was getting bad. His coat had taken on a few more faded shades of color, the twine strings were more frayed and ragged, the last remaining button — the button of yellow horn — was gone. A motley descendant of kings was Uncle Cæsar!

About two hours later I saw an excited crowd besieging the front of the drug store. In a desert where nothing happens this was manna; so I wedged my way inside. On an extemporized couch of empty boxes and chairs was stretched the mortal corporeality of Major Wentworth Caswell. A doctor was testing him for the mortal ingredient. His decision was that it was conspicuous by its absence.

The erstwhile Major had been found dead on a dark street and brought by curious and ennuied citizens to the drug store. The late human being had been engaged in terrific battle — the details showed that. Loafer and reprobate though he had been, he had been also a warrior. But he had lost. His hands were yet clenched so tightly that his fingers would not be opened. The gentle citizens who had known him stood about and searched their vocabularies to find some good words, if it were possible, to speak of him. One kind-looking man said, after much thought: "When 'Cas' was about fo'teen he was one of the best spellers in the school."

While I stood there the fingers of the right hand of "the man that was," which hung down the side of a white pine box, relaxed, and dropped something at my feet. I covered it with one foot quietly, and a little later on I picked it up and pocketed it. I reasoned that in his last struggle his hand must have seized that object unwittingly and held it in a death grip.

At the hotel that night the main topic of conversation, with the possible exceptions of politics and prohibition, was the demise of Major Caswell. I heard one man say to a group of listeners:

"In my opinion, gentlemen, Caswell was murdered by some of these no-account niggars for his money. He had fifty dollars this afternoon which he showed to several gentlemen in the hotel. When he was found the money was not on his person."

I left the city the next morning at nine, and as the train was crossing the bridge over the Cumberland River I took out of my pocket a yellow horn overcoat button the size of a fifty-cent piece, with frayed ends of coarse twine hanging from it, and cast it out of the window into the slow, muddy waters below.

I wonder what's doing in Buffalo!

THE DISSIPATED JEWELER

You will not find the name of Thomas Keeling in the Houston city directory. It might have been there by this time, if Mr. Keeling had not discontinued his business a month or so ago and moved to other parts. Mr. Keeling came to Houston about that time and opened up a small detective bureau. He offered his services to the public as a detective in rather a modest way. He did not aspire to be a rival of the Pinkerton agency, but preferred to work along less risky lines.

If an employer wanted the habits of a clerk looked into, or a lady wanted an eye kept upon a somewhat too gay husband, Mr. Keeling was the man to take the job. He was a quiet, studious man with theories. He read Gaboriau and Conan Doyle and hoped some day to take a higher place in his profession. He had held a subordinate place in a large detective bureau in the East, but as promotion was slow, he decided to come West, where the field was not so well covered.

Mr. Keeling had saved during several years the sum of $900, which he deposited in the safe of a business man in Houston to whom he had letters of introduction from a common friend. He rented a small upstairs office on an obscure street, hung out a sign stating his business, and burying himself in one of Doyle's Sherlock Holmes stories, waited for customers.

Three days after he opened his bureau, which consisted of himself, a client called to see him.

It was a young lady, apparently about 26 years of age. She was slender and rather tall and neatly dressed. She wore a thin veil which she threw back upon her black straw hat after she had taken the chair Mr. Keeling offered her. She had a delicate, refined face, with rather quick gray eyes, and a slightly nervous manner.

"I came to see you, sir," she said in a sweet, but somewhat sad, contralto voice, "because you are comparatively a stranger, and I could not bear to discuss my private affairs with any of my friends. I desire to employ you to watch the movements of my husband. Humiliating as the confession is to me, I fear that his affections are no longer mine. Before I married him he was infatuated with a young woman connected with a family with whom he boarded. We have been married five years, and very happily, but this young woman has recently moved to Houston, and I have reasons to suspect that he is paying her attentions. I want you to watch his movements as closely as possible and re-

31

port to me. I will call here at your office every other day at a given time to learn what you have discovered. My name is Mrs. R——, and my husband is well known. He keeps a small jewelry store on —— Street. I will pay you well for your services and here is $20 to begin with."

The lady handed Mr. Keeling the bill and he took it carelessly as if such things were very, very common in his business. He assured her that he would carry out her wishes faithfully, and asked her to call again the afternoon after the next at four o'clock, for the first report.

The next day Mr. Keeling made the necessary inquiries toward beginning operations. He found the jewelry store, and went inside ostensibly to have the crystal of his watch tightened. The jeweler, Mr. R ——, was a man apparently 35 years of age, of very quiet manners and industrious ways. His store was small, but contained a nice selection of goods and quite a large assortment of diamonds, jewelry and watches. Further inquiry elicited the information that Mr. R—— was a man of excellent habits, never drank and was always at work at his jeweler's bench.

Mr. Keeling loafed around near the door of the jewelry store for several hours that day and was finally rewarded by seeing a flashily dressed young woman with black hair and eyes enter the store. Mr. Keeling sauntered nearer the door, where he could see what took place inside. The young woman walked confidently to the rear of the store, leaned over the counter and spoke familiarly to Mr. R —— He rose from his bench and they talked in low tones for a few minutes. Finally the jeweler handed her some coins, which Mr. Keeling heard clinking as they passed into her hands. The woman then came out and walked rapidly down the street.

Mr. Keeling's client was at his office promptly at the time agreed upon. She was anxious to know if he had seen anything to corroborate her suspicions. The detective told her what he had seen.

"That is she," said the lady, when he had described the young woman who had entered the store. "The brazen, bold thing! And so Charles is giving her money. To think that things should come to this pass."

The lady pressed her handkerchief to her eyes in an agitated way.

"Mrs. R ——," said the detective, "what is your desire in this matter? To what point do you wish me to prosecute inquiries?"

"I want to see with my own eyes enough to convince me of what I suspect. I also want witnesses, so I can instigate suit for divorce. I will not lead the life I am now living any longer."

She then handed the detective a ten-dollar bill.

On the day following the next, when she came to Mr. Keeling's office to hear his report, he said:

"I dropped into the store this afternoon on some trifling pretext. This young woman was already there, but she did not remain long. Before she left, she said: 'Charlie, we will have a jolly little supper tonight as you suggest; then we will come around to the store and have a nice chat while you finish that setting for the diamond brooch with no one to interrupt us.' Tonight, Mrs. R——, I think, will be a good time for you to witness the meeting between your husband and the object of his infatuation, and satisfy your mind how matters stand."

"The wretch," cried the lady with flashing eyes. "He told me at dinner that he would be detained late tonight with some important work. And this is the way he spends his time away from me!"

"I suggest," said the detective, "that you conceal yourself in the store, so you can hear what they say, and when you have heard enough you can summon witnesses and confront your husband before them."

"The very thing," said the lady. "I believe there is a policeman whose beat is along the street the store is on who is acquainted with our family. His duties will lead him to be in the vicinity of the store after dark. Why not see him, explain the whole matter to him and when I have heard enough, let you and him appear as witnesses?"

"I will speak with him," said the detective, "and persuade him to assist us, and you will please come to my office a little before dark tonight, so we can arrange to trap them."

The detective hunted up the policeman and explained the situation.

"That's funny," said the guardian of the peace. "I didn't know R —— was a gay boy at all. But, then, you can never tell about anybody. So his wife wants to catch him tonight. Let's see, she wants to hide herself inside the store and hear what they say. There's a little room in the back of the store where R —— keeps his coal and old boxes. The door between is locked, of course, but if you can get her through that into the store she can hide somewhere. I don't like to mix up in these affairs, but I sympathize with the lady. I've known her ever since we were children and don't mind helping her to do what she wants."

About dusk that evening the detective's client came hurriedly to his office. She was dressed plainly in black and wore a dark round hat and her face was covered with a veil.

"If Charlie should see me he will not recognize me," she said.

Mr. Keeling and the lady strolled down the street opposite the jewelry store, and about eight o'clock the young woman they were watch-

ing for entered the store. Immediately afterwards she came out with
Mr. R ——, took his arm, and they hurried away, presumably to their
supper.

The detective felt the arm of the lady tremble.

"The wretch," she said bitterly. "He thinks me at home innocently
waiting for him while he is out carousing with that artful, designing
minx. Oh, the perfidy of man."

Mr. Keeling took the lady through an open hallway that led into
the back yard of the store. The outer door of the back room was un-
locked, and they entered.

"In the store," said Mrs. R——, "near the bench where my husband
works is a large table, the cover of which hangs to the floor. If I could
get under that I could hear every word that was said."

Mr. Keeling took a big bunch of skeleton keys from his pocket and
in a few minutes found one that opened the door into the jewelry
store. The gas was burning from one jet turned very low.

The lady stepped into the store and said: "I will bolt this door from
the inside, and I want you to follow my husband and that woman. See
if they are at supper, and if they are, when they start back, you must
come back to this room and let me know by tapping thrice on the door.
After I listen to their conversation long enough I will unbolt the door,
and we will confront the guilty pair together. I may need you to pro-
tect me, for I do not know what they might attempt to do to me."

The detective made his way softly out and followed the jeweler and
the woman. He soon discovered that they had taken a private room in
a little out of the way restaurant and had ordered supper. He lingered
about until they came out and then hurried back to the store, and
entering the back room, tapped three times on the door.

In a few minutes the jeweler entered with the woman and the detective saw the light shine more brightly through a crack in the door. He
could hear the man and woman conversing familiarly and constantly,
but could not distinguish their words. He slipped around again to the
street, and looking through the window, could see Mr. R—— working
away at his jeweler's bench, while the black-haired woman sat close to
his side and talked.

"I'll give them a little time," thought Mr. Keeling, and he strolled
down the street.

The policeman was standing on the corner.

The detective told him that Mrs. R—— was concealed in the store,
and that the scheme was working nicely.

"I'll drop back behind now," said Mr. Keeling, "so as to be ready when the lady springs her trap."

The policeman walked back with him, and took a look through the window.

"They seem to have made up all right," said he. "Where's the other woman gotten to?"

"Why, there she is sitting by him," said the detective.

"I'm talking about the girl R —— had out to supper."

"So am I," said the detective.

"You seem to be mixed up," said the policeman. "Do you know that lady with R ——?"

"That's the woman he was out with."

"That's R——'s wife," said the policeman. "I've known her for fifteen years."

"Then, who ——?" gasped the detective, "Lord A'mighty, then who's under the table?"

Mr. Keeling began to kick at the door of the store.

Mr. R —— came forward and opened it. The policeman and the detective entered.

"Look under that table, quick," yelled the detective. The policeman raised the cover and dragged out a black dress, a black veil and a woman's wig of black hair.

"Is this lady your w-w-wife?" asked Mr. Keeling excitedly, pointing out the dark-eyed young woman, who was regarding them in great surprise.

"Certainly," said the jeweler. "Now what the thunder are you looking under my tables and kicking down my door for, if you please?"

"Look in your show cases," said the policeman, who began to size up the situation.

The diamond rings and watches that were missing amounted to $800; and the next day the detective settled the bill.

Explanations were made to the jeweler that night, and an hour later Mr. Keeling sat in his office busily engaged in looking over his albums of crook's photos.

At last he found one, and he stopped turning over the leaves and tore his hair. Under the picture of a smooth-faced young man, with delicate features was the following description:

"James H. Miggles, alias Slick Simon, alias The Weeping Widow, alias Bunco Kate, alias Jimmy the Sneak. General confidence man and burglar. Works generally in female disguises. Very plausible and dan-

gerous. Wanted in Kansas City, Oshkosh, New Orleans and Milwau-
kee."

This is why Mr. Thomas Keeling did not continue his detective
business in Houston.

THE ADVENTURES OF SHAMROCK JOLNES

I AM so fortunate as to count Shamrock Jolnes, the great New York detective, among my muster of friends. Jolnes is what is called the "inside man" of the city detective force. He is an expert in the use of the typewriter, and it is his duty, whenever there is a "murder mystery" to be solved, to sit at a desk telephone at headquarters and take down the messages of "cranks" who 'phone in their confessions to having committed the crime.

But on certain "off" days when confessions are coming in slowly and three or four newspapers have run to earth as many different guilty persons, Jolnes will knock about the town with me, exhibiting, to my great delight and instruction, his marvellous powers of observation and deduction.

The other day I dropped in at Headquarters and found the great detective gazing thoughtfully at a string that was tied tightly around his little finger.

"Good morning, Whatsup," he said, without turning his head. "I'm glad to notice that you've had your house fitted up with electric lights at last."

"Will you please tell me," I said, in surprise, "how you knew that? I am sure that I never mentioned the fact to any one, and the wiring was a rush order not completed until this morning."

"Nothing easier," said Jolnes, genially. "As you came in I caught the odor of the cigar you are smoking. I know an expensive cigar; and I know that not more than three men in New York can afford to smoke cigars and pay gas bills too at the present time. That was an easy one. But I am working just now on a little problem of my own."

"Why have you that string on your finger?" I asked.

"That's the problem," said Jolnes. "My wife tied that on this morning to remind me of something I was to send up to the house. Sit down, Whatsup, and excuse me for a few moments."

The distinguished detective went to a walk telephone, and stood with the receiver to his ear for probably ten minutes.

"Were you listening to a confession?" I asked, when he had returned to his chair.

"Perhaps," said Jolnes, with a smile, "it might be called something of the sort. To be frank with you, Whatsup, I've cut out the dope. I've been increasing the quantity for so long that morphine doesn't have

much effect on me any more. I've got to have something more powerful. That telephone I just went to is connected with a room in the
Waldorf where there's an author's reading in progress. Now, to get
at the solution of this string."

After five minutes of silent pondering, Jolnes looked at me, with a
smile, and nodded his head.

"Wonderful man!" I exclaimed; "already?"

"It is quite simple," he said, holding up his finger. "You see that
knot? That is to prevent my forgetting. It is, therefore, a forget-me-
knot. A forget-me-not is a flower. It was a sack of flour that I was to
send home!"

"Beautiful!" I could not help crying out in admiration.

"Suppose we go out for a ramble," suggested Jolnes.

"There is only one case of importance on hand now. Old man Mc-
Carty, one hundred and four years old, died from eating too many
bananas. The evidence points so strongly to the Mafia that the police
have surrounded the Second Avenue Katzenjammer Gambrinus Club
No. 2, and the capture of the assassin is only the matter of a few hours.
The detective force has not yet been called on for assistance."

Jolnes and I went out and up the street toward the corner, where
we were to catch a surface car.

Halfway up the block we met Rheingelder, an acquaintance of
ours, who held a City Hall position.

"Good morning, Rheingelder," said Jolnes, halting. "Nice breakfast that was you had this morning."

Always on the lookout for the detective's remarkable feats of deduction, I saw Jolnes's eyes flash for an instant upon a long yellow
splash on the shirt bosom and a smaller one upon the chin of Rheingelder — both undoubtedly made by the yolk of an egg.

"Oh, dot is some of your detectiveness," said Rheingelder, shaking
all over with a smile. "Vell, I bet you trinks and cigars all around dot
you cannot tell vot I haf eaten for breakfast."

"Done," said Jolnes. "Sausage, pumpernickel, and coffee."

Rheingelder admitted the correctness of the surmise and paid the
bet. When we had proceeded on our way I said to Jolnes:

"I thought you looked at the egg spilled on his chin and shirt front."

"I did," said Jolnes. "That is where I began my deduction. Rheingelder is a very economical, saving man. Yesterday eggs dropped in the
market to twenty-eight cents per dozen. To-day they are quoted at
forty-two. Rheingelder ate eggs yesterday, and to-day he went back to
his usual fare. A little thing like this isn't anything, Whatsup; it be-

longs to the primary arithmetic class."

When we boarded the street car we found the seats all occupied — principally by ladies. Jolnes and I stood on the rear platform.

About the middle of the car there sat an elderly man with a short, gray beard, who looked to be the typical, well-dressed New Yorker. At successive corners other ladies climbed aboard, and soon three or four of them were standing over the man, clinging to straps and glaring meaningly at the man who occupied the coveted seat. But he resolutely retained his place.

"We New Yorkers," I remarked to Jolnes, "have about lost our manners, as far as the exercise of them in public goes."

"Perhaps so," said Jolnes, lightly; "but the man you evidently refer to happens to be a very chivalrous and courteous gentleman from Old Virginia. He is spending a few days in New York with his wife and two daughters, and he leaves for the South to-night."

"You know him, then?" I said, in amazement.

"I never saw him before we stepped on the car," declared the detective, smilingly.

"By the gold tooth of the Witch of Endor!" I cried, "if you can construe all that from his appearance you are dealing in nothing else than black art."

"The habit of observation — nothing more," said Jolnes. "If the old gentleman gets off the car before we do, I think I can demonstrate to you the accuracy of my deduction."

Three blocks farther along the gentleman rose to leave the car. Jolnes addressed him at the door:

"Pardon me, sir, but are you not Colonel Hunter, of Norfolk, Virginia?"

"No, suh," was the extremely courteous answer. "My name, suh, is Ellison — Major Winfield R. Ellison, from Fairfax County, in the same state. I know a good many people, suh, in Norfolk — the Goodriches, the Tollivers, and the Crabtrees, suh, but I never had the pleasure of meeting yo' friend, Colonel Hunter. I am happy to say, suh, that I am going back to Virginia to-night, after having spent a week in yo' city with my wife and three daughters. I shall be in Norfolk in about ten days, and if you will give me yo' name, suh, I will take pleasure in looking up Colonel Hunter and telling him that you inquired after him, suh."

"Thank you," said Jolnes; "tell him that Reynolds sent his regards, if you will be so kind."

I glanced at the great New York detective and saw that a look of intense chagrin had come upon his clear-cut features. Failure in the slightest point always galled Shamrock Jolnes.

"Did you say your *three* daughters?" he asked of the Virginia gentleman.

"Yes, suh, my three daughters, all as fine girls as there are in Fairfax County," was the answer.

With that Major Ellison stopped the car and began to descend the step.

Shamrock Jolnes clutched his arm.

"One moment, sir," he begged, in an urbane voice in which I alone detected the anxiety — "am I not right in believing that one of the young ladies is an *adopted* daughter?"

"You are, suh," admitted the major, from the ground, "but how the devil you knew it, suh, is mo' than I can tell."

"And mo' than I can tell, too," I said, as the car went on.

Jolnes was restored to his calm, observant serenity by having wrested victory from his apparent failure; so after we got off the car he invited me into a café promising to reveal the process of his latest wonderful feat.

"In the first place," he began after we were comfortably seated, "I knew the gentleman was no New Yorker because he was flushed and uneasy and restless on account of the ladies that were standing, although he did not rise and give them his seat. I decided from his appearance that he was a Southerner rather than a Westerner.

"Next I began to figure out his reason for not relinquishing his seat to a lady when he evidently felt strongly, but not overpoweringly, impelled to do so. I very quickly decided upon that. I noticed that one of his eyes had received a severe jab in one corner, which was red and inflamed, and that all over his face were tiny round marks about the size of the end of an uncut lead pencil. Also upon both of his patent-leather shoes were a number of deep imprints shaped like ovals cut off square at one end.

"Now, there is only one district in New York City where a man is bound to receive scars and wounds and indentations of that sort — and that is along the sidewalks of Twenty-third Street and a portion of Sixth Avenue south of there. I knew from the imprints of trampling French heels on his feet and the marks of countless jabs in the face from umbrellas and parasols carried by women in the shopping district that he had been in conflict with the Amazonian troops. And as he was a man of intelligent appearance, I knew he would not have braved such dangers unless he had been dragged thither by his own women folk. Therefore, when he got on the car his anger at the treatment he had received was sufficient to make him keep his seat in spite of his traditions of Southern chivalry."

"That is all very well," I said, "but why did you insist upon daughters — and especially two daughters? Why couldn't a wife alone have taken him shopping?"

"There had to be daughters," said Jolnes, calmly. "If he had only a wife, and she near his own age, he could have bluffed her into going alone. If he had a young wife she would prefer to go alone. So there you are."

"I'll admit that," I said; "but, now, why two daughters? And how, in the name of all the prophets, did you guess that one was adopted when he told you he had three?"

"Don't say guess," said Jolnes, with a touch of pride in his air; "there is no such word in the lexicon of ratiocination. In Major Ellison's buttonhole there was a carnation and a rosebud backed by a geranium leaf. No woman ever combined a carnation and a rosebud into a boutonniere. Close your eyes, Whatsup, and give the logic of imagination a chance. Cannot you see the lovely Adele fastening the carnation to the lapel so that papa may be gay upon the street? And then the romping Edith May dancing up with sisterly jealousy to add her rosebud to the adornment?"

"And then," I cried, beginning to feel enthusiasm, "when he declared that he had three daughters ——"

"I could see," said Jolnes, "one in the background who added no flower; and I knew that she must be ——"

"Adopted!" I broke in. "I give you every credit; but how did you know he was leaving for the South to-night?"

"In his breast pocket," said the great detective, "something large and oval made a protuberance. Good liquor is scarce on trains, and it is a long journey from New York to Fairfax County."

"Again, I must bow to you," I said. "And tell me this, so that my last shred of doubt will be cleared away; why did you decide that he was from Virginia?"

"It was very faint, I admit," answered Shamrock Jones, "but no trained observer could have failed to detect the odor of mint in the car."

THE COP AND THE ANTHEM

On his bench in Madison Square Soapy moved uneasily. When wild geese honk high of nights, and when women without sealskin coats grow kind to their husbands, and when Soapy moves uneasily on his bench in the park, you may know that winter is near at hand.

A dead leaf fell in Soapy's lap. That was Jack Frost's card. Jack is kind to the regular denizens of Madison Square, and gives fair warning of his annual call. At the corners of four streets he hands his pasteboard to the North Wind, footman of the mansion of All Outdoors, so that the inhabitants thereof may make ready.

Soapy's mind became cognizant of the fact that the time had come for him to resolve himself into a singular Committee of Ways and Means to provide against the coming rigor. And therefore he moved uneasily on his bench.

The hibernatorial ambitions of Soapy were not of the highest. In them were no considerations of Mediterranean cruises, of soporific Southern skies or drifting in the Vesuvian Bay. Three months on the Island was what his soul craved. Three months of assured board and bed and congenial company, safe from Boreas and bluecoats, seemed to Soapy the essence of things desirable.

For years the hospitable Blackwell's had been his winter quarters. Just as his more fortunate fellow New Yorkers had bought their tickets to Palm Beach and the Riviera each winter, so Soapy had made his humble arrangements for his annual hegira to the Island. And now the time was come. On the previous night three Sabbath newspapers, distributed beneath his coat, about his ankles and over his lap, had failed to repulse the cold as he slept on his bench near the spurting fountain in the ancient square. So the Island loomed big and timely in Soapy's mind. He scorned the provisions made in the name of charity for the city's dependents. In Soapy's opinion the Law was more benign than Philanthropy. There was an endless round of institutions, municipal and eleemosynary, on which he might set out and receive lodging and food accordant with the simple life. But to one of Soapy's proud spirit the gifts of charity are encumbered. If not in coin you must pay in humiliation of spirit for every benefit received at the hands of philanthropy. As Cæsar had his Brutus, every bed of charity must have its toll of a bath, every loaf of bread its compensation of a private and personal inquisition. Wherefore it is better to be a guest of the law, which, though conducted by rules, does not meddle unduly with a gentleman's private affairs.

Soapy, having decided to go to the Island, at once set about accomplishing his desire. There were many easy ways of doing this. The pleasantest was to dine luxuriously at some expensive restaurant; and then, after declaring insolvency, be handed over quietly and without uproar to a policeman. An accommodating magistrate would do the rest.

Soapy left his bench and strolled out of the square and across the level sea of asphalt, where Broadway and Fifth Avenue flow together. Up Broadway he turned, and halted at a glittering café, where are gathered together nightly the choicest products of the grape, the silkworm, and the protoplasm.

Soapy had confidence in himself from the lowest button of his vest upward. He was shaven, and his coat was decent and his neat black, ready-tied four-in-hand had been presented to him by a lady missionary on Thanksgiving Day. If he could reach a table in the restaurant unsuspected success would be his. The portion of him that would show above the table would raise no doubt in the waiter's mind. A roasted mallard duck, thought Soapy, would be about the thing — with a bottle of Chablis, and then Camembert, a demi-tasse and a cigar. One dollar for the cigar would be enough. The total would not be so high as to call forth any supreme manifestation of revenge from the café management; and yet the meal would leave him filled and happy for the journey to his winter refuge.

But as Soapy set foot inside the restaurant door the head waiter's eye fell upon his frayed trousers and decadent shoes. Strong and ready hands turned him about and conveyed him in silence and haste to the sidewalk and averted the ignoble fate of the menaced mallard.

Soapy turned off Broadway. It seemed that his route to the coveted Island was not to be an epicurean one. Some other way of entering limbo must be thought of.

At a corner of Sixth Avenue electric lights and cunningly displayed wares behind plate-glass made a shop window conspicuous. Soapy took a cobblestone and dashed it through the glass. People came running around the corner, a policeman in the lead. Soapy stood still, with his hands in his pockets, and smiled at the sight of brass buttons.

"Where's the man that done that?" inquired the officer, excitedly.

"Don't you figure out that I might have had something to do with it?" said Soapy, not without sarcasm, but friendly, as one greets good fortune.

The policeman's mind refused to accept Soapy even as a clue. Men who smash windows do not remain to parley with the law's minions. They take to their heels. The policeman saw a man halfway down the block running to catch a car. With drawn club he joined in the pursuit, Soapy, with disgust in his heart, loafed along, twice unsuccessful.

On the opposite side of the street was a restaurant of no great pretensions. It catered to large appetites and modest purses. Its crockery and atmosphere were thick; its soup and napery thin. Into this place Soapy took his accusive shoes and telltale trousers without challenge. At a table he sat and consumed beefsteak, flapjacks, doughnuts and pie. And then to the waiter he betrayed the fact that the minutest coin and himself were strangers.

"Now, get busy and call a cop," said Soapy. "And don't keep a gentleman waiting."

"No cop for youse," said the waiter, with a voice like butter cakes and an eye like the cherry in a Manhattan cocktail. "Hey, Con!"

Neatly upon his left ear on the callous pavement two waiters pitched Soapy. He arose joint by joint, as a carpenter's rule opens, and beat the dust from his clothes. Arrest seemed but a rosy dream. The Island seemed very far away. A policeman who stood before a drug store two doors away laughed and walked down the street.

Five blocks Soapy travelled before his courage permitted him to woo capture again. This time the opportunity presented what he fatuously termed to himself a "cinch." A young woman of a modest and pleasing guise was standing before a show window gazing with sprightly interest at its display of shaving mugs and inkstands, and two yards from the window a large policeman of severe demeanor leaned against a water plug.

It was Soapy's design to assume the rôle of the despicable and execrated "masher." The refined and elegant appearance of his victim and the contiguity of the conscientious cop encouraged him to believe that he would soon feel the pleasant official clutch upon his arm that would insure his winter quarters on the right little, tight little isle.

Soapy straightened the lady missionary's ready-made tie, dragged his shrinking cuffs into the open, set his hat at a killing cant and sidled toward the young woman. He made eyes at her, was taken with sudden coughs and "hems," smiled, smirked and went brazenly through the impudent and contemptible litany of the "masher." With half an eye Soapy saw that the policeman was watching him fixedly. The young woman moved away a few steps, and again bestowed her absorbed attention upon the shaving mugs. Soapy followed, boldly stepping to her side, raised his hat and said:

'Ah there, Bedelia! Don't you want to come and play in my yard?"

The policeman was still looking. The persecuted young woman had but to beckon a finger and Soapy would be practically en route for his insular haven. Already he imagined he could feel the cozy warmth of the station-house. The young woman faced him and, stretching out a hand, caught Soapy's coat sleeve.

"Sure, Mike," she said, joyfully, "if you'll blow me to a pail of suds. I'd have spoke to you sooner, but the cop was watching."

With the young woman playing the clinging ivy to his oak Soapy walked past the policeman overcome with gloom. He seemed doomed to liberty.

At the next corner he shook off his companion and ran. He halted in the district where by night are found the lightest streets, hearts, vows and librettos. Women in furs and men in greatcoats moved gaily in the wintry air. A sudden fear seized Soapy that some dreadful enchantment had rendered him immune to arrest. The thought brought a little panic upon it, and when he came upon another policeman lounging grandly in front of a transplendent theatre he caught at the immediate straw of "disorderly conduct."

On the sidewalk Soapy began to yell drunken gibberish at the top of his harsh voice. He danced, howled, raved, and otherwise disturbed the welkin.

The policeman twirled his club, turned his back to Soapy and remarked to a citizen.

" 'Tis one of them Yale lads celebratin' the goose egg they give to the Hartford College. Noisy; but no harm. We've instructions to leave them be."

Disconsolate, Soapy ceased his unavailing racket. Would never a policeman lay hands on him? In his fancy the Island seemed an unattainable Arcadia. He buttoned his thin coat against the chilling wind.

In a cigar store he saw a well-dressed man lighting a cigar at a swinging light. His silk umbrella he had set by the door on entering. Soapy stepped inside, secured the umbrella and sauntered off with it slowly. The man at the cigar light followed hastily.

"My umbrella," he said, sternly.

"Oh, is it?" sneered Soapy, adding insult to petit larceny. "Well, why don't you call a policeman? I took it. Your umbrella! Why don't you call a cop? There stands one on the corner."

The umbrella owner slowed his steps. Soapy did likewise, with a presentiment that luck would again run against him. The policeman looked at the two curiously.

"Of course," said the umbrella man — "that is — well, you know how these mistakes occur — I — if it's your umbrella I hope you'll excuse me — I picked it up this morning in a restaurant — If you recognize it as yours, why — I hope you'll ——"

"Of course it's mine," said Soapy, viciously.

The ex-umbrella man retreated. The policeman hurried to assist a tall blonde in an opera cloak across the street in front of a street car that was approaching two blocks away.

Soapy walked eastward through a street damaged by improvements. He hurled the umbrella wrathfully into an excavation. He muttered against the men who wear helmets and carry clubs. Because he wanted to fall into their clutches, they seemed to regard him as a king who could do no wrong.

At length Soapy reached one of the avenues to the east where the glitter and turmoil was but faint. He set his face down this toward Madison Square, for the homing instinct survives even when the home is a park bench.

But on an unusually quiet corner Soapy came to a standstill. Here was an old church, quaint and rambling and gabled. Through one violet-stained window a soft light glowed, where, no doubt, the organist loitered over the keys, making sure of his mastery of the coming Sabbath anthem. For there drifted out to Soapy's ears sweet music that caught and held him transfixed against the convolutions of the iron fence.

The moon was above, lustrous and serene; vehicles and pedestrians were few; sparrows twittered sleepily in the eaves — for a little while the scene might have been a country churchyard. And the anthem that the organist played cemented Soapy to the iron fence, for he had known it well in the days when his life contained such things as mothers and roses and ambitions and friends and immaculate thoughts and collars.

The conjunction of Soapy's receptive state of mind and the influences about the old church wrought a sudden and wonderful change in his soul. He viewed with swift horror the pit into which he had tumbled, the degraded days, unworthy desires, dead hopes, wrecked faculties and base motives that made up his existence.

And also in a moment his heart responded thrillingly to this novel mood. An instantaneous and strong impulse moved him to battle with his desperate fate. He would pull himself out of the mire; he would make a man of himself again; he would conquer the evil that had taken possession of him. There was time; he was comparatively young yet; he would resurrect his old eager ambitions and pursue them without faltering. Those solemn but sweet organ notes had set up a revolution in him. To-morrow he would go into the roaring downtown district and find work. A fur importer had once offered him a place as a driver. He would find him to-morrow and ask for the position. He would be somebody in the world. He would ——

Soapy felt a hand laid on his arm. He looked quickly around into the broad face of a policeman.

"What are you doin' here?" asked the officer.

"Nothin'," said Soapy.

"Then come along," said the policeman.

"Three months on the Island," said the Magistrate in the Police Court the next morning.

JEFF PETERS AS A PERSONAL MAGNET

JEFF PETERS has been engaged in as many schemes for making money as there are recipes for cooking rice in Charleston, S. C.

Best of all I like to hear him tell of his earlier days when he sold liniments and cough cures on street corners, living hand to mouth, heart to heart with the people, throwing heads or tails with fortune for his last coin.

"I struck Fisher Hill, Arkansas," said he, "in buckskin suit, moccasins, long hair and a thirty-carat diamond ring that I got from an actor in Texarkana. I don't know what he ever did with the pocket knife I swapped him for it.

"I was Dr. Waugh-hoo, the celebrated Indian medicine man. I carried only one best bet just then, and that was Resurrection Bitters. It was made of life-giving plants and herbs accidentally discovered by Ta-qua-la, the beautiful wife of the chief of the Choctaw Nation, while gathering truck to garnish a platter of boiled dog for the annual corn dance.

"Business hadn't been good at the last town, so I only had five dollars. I went to the Fisher Hill druggist and he credited me for a half gross of eight ounce bottles and corks. I had the labels and ingredients in my valise, left over from the last town. Life began to look rosy again after I got in my hotel room with the water running from the tap, and the Resurrection Bitters lining up on the table by the dozen.

"Fake? No, sir. There was two dollars' worth of fluid extract of cinchona and a dime's worth of aniline in that half-gross of bitters. I've gone through towns years afterwards and had folks ask for 'em again.

"I hired a wagon that night and commenced selling the bitters on Main Street. Fisher Hill was a low, malarial town; and a compound hypothetical pneumo-cardiac anti-scorbutic tonic was just what I diagnosed the crowd as needing. The bitters started off like sweetbreads-on-toast at a vegetarian dinner. I had sold two dozen at fifty cents apiece when I felt somebody pull my coat tail. I knew what that meant; so I climbed down and sneaked a five-dollar bill into the hand of a man with a German silver star on his lapel.

" 'Constable,' says I, 'it's a fine night.'

" 'Have you got a city license,' he asks, 'to sell this illegitimate essence of spooju that you flatter by the name of medicine?'

" 'I have not,' says I. 'I didn't know you had a city. If I can find it tomorrow I'll take one out if it's necessary.'

" 'I'll have to close you up till you do,' says the constable.

"I quit selling and went back to the hotel. I was talking to the land-lord about it.

" 'Oh, you won't stand no show in Fisher Hill,' says he. 'Dr. Hos-kins, the only doctor here, is a brother-in-law of the Mayor, and they won't allow no fake doctors to practice in town.'

" 'I don't practice medicine,' says I, 'I've got a State peddler's li-cense, and I take out a city one wherever they demand it.'

"I went to the Mayor's office the next morning and they told me he hadn't showed up yet. They didn't know when he'd be down. So Doc Waugh-hoo hunches down again in a hotel chair and lights a jimpson-weed regalia, and waits.

"By and by a young man in a blue necktie slips into the chair next to me and asks the time.

" 'Half-past ten,' says I, 'and you are Andy Tucker. I've seen you work. Wasn't it you that put up the Great Cupid Combination pack-age on the Southern States? Let's see, it was a Chilian diamond en-gagement ring, a wedding ring, a potato masher, a bottle of soothing syrup and Dorothy Vernon — all for fifty cents.'

"Andy was pleased to hear that I remembered him. He was a good street man; and he was more than that — he respected his profession, and he was satisfied with 300 per cent profit. He had plenty of offers to go into the illegitimate drug and garden seed business; but he was never to be tempted off of the straight path.

"I wanted a partner, so Andy and me agreed to go out together. I told him about the situation on Fisher Hill and how finances was low on account of the local mixture of politics and jalap. Andy had just got in on the train that morning. He was pretty low himself, and was going to canvass the town for a few dollars to build a new battleship by popular subscription at Eureka Springs. So we went out and sat on the porch and talked it over.

"The next morning at eleven o'clock when I was sitting there alone, an Uncle Tom shuffles into the hotel and asked for the doctor to come and see Judge Banks, who, it seems, was the mayor and a mighty sick man.

" 'I'm no doctor,' says I. 'Why don't you go and get the doctor?'

" 'Boss,' says he. 'Doc Hoskin am done gone twenty miles in the country to see some sick persons. He's de only doctor in de town, and Massa Banks am powerful bad off. He sent me to ax you to please, suh, come.'

" 'As man to man,' says I, 'I'll go and look him over.' So I put a bottle of Resurrection Bitters in my pocket and goes up on the hill to the mayor's mansion, the finest house in town, with a mansard roof and two cast-iron dogs on the lawn.

"This Mayor Banks was in bed all but his whiskers and feet. He was making internal noises that would have had everybody in San Francisco hiking for the parks. A young man was standing by the bed holding a cup of water.

" 'Doc,' says the Mayor, 'I'm awful sick. I'm about to die. Can't you do nothing for me?'

" 'Mr. Mayor,' says I, 'I'm not a regular preordained disciple of S. Q. Lapius. I never took a course in a medical college,' says I. 'I've just come as a fellow man to see if I could be of any assistance.'

" 'I'm deeply obliged,' says he. 'Doc Waugh-hoo, this is my nephew, Mr. Biddle. He has tried to alleviate my distress, but without success. Oh, Lordy! Ow-ow-ow! !' he sings out.

"I nods at Mr. Biddle and sets down by the bed and feels the mayor's pulse. 'Let me see your liver — your tongue, I mean,' says I. Then I turns up the lids of his eyes and looks close at the pupils of 'em.

" 'How long have you been sick?' I asked.

" 'I was taken down — ow-ouch — last night,' says the Mayor. 'Gimme something for it, doc, won't you?'

" 'Mr. Fiddle,' says I, 'raise the window shade a bit, will you?'

" 'Biddle,' says the young man. 'Do you feel like you could eat some ham and eggs, Uncle James?'

" 'Mr. Mayor,' says I, after laying my ear to his right shoulder blade and listening, 'you've got a bad attack of super-inflammation of the right clavicle of the harpischord!'

" 'Good Lord!' says he, with a groan. 'Can't you rub something on it, or set it or anything?'

"I picks up my hat and starts for the door.

" 'You ain't going, doc?' says the Mayor with a howl. 'You ain't going away and leave me to die with this — superfluity of the clapboards, are you?'

" 'Common humanity, Dr. Whoa-ha,' says Mr. Biddle, 'ought to prevent your deserting a fellow-human in distress.'

" 'Dr. Waugh-hoo, when you get through plowing,' says I. And then I walks back to the bed and throws back my long hair.

" 'Mr. Mayor,' says I, 'there is only one hope for you. Drugs will do you no good. But there is another power higher yet, although drugs are high enough,' says I.

'And what is that?' says he.

" 'Scientific demonstrations,' says I. 'The triumph of mind over sarsaparilla. The belief that there is no pain and sickness except what is produced when we ain't feeling well. Declare yourself in arrears. Demonstrate.'

" 'What is this paraphernalia you speak of, Doc?' says the Mayor. 'You ain't a Socialist, are you?'

" 'I am speaking,' says I, 'of the great doctrine of psychic financiering — of the enlightened school of long-distance, sub-conscientious treatment of fallacies and meningitis — of that wonderful in-door sport known as personal magnetism.'

" 'Can you work it, Doc?' asks the Mayor.

" 'I'm one of the Sole Sanhedrims and Ostensible Hooplas of the Inner Pulpit,' says I. 'The lame walk and the blind rubber whenever I make a pass at 'em. I am a medium, a coloratura hypnotist and a spirituous control. It was only through me at the recent seances at Ann Arbor that the late president of the Vinegar Bitters Company could revisit the earth to communicate with his sister Jane. You see me peddling medicine on the streets,' says I, 'to the poor. I don't practice personal magnetism on them. I do not drag it in the dust,' says I, 'because they haven't got the dust.'

" 'Will you treat my case?' asks the Mayor.

" 'Listen,' says I. 'I've had a good deal of trouble with medical societies everywhere I've been. I don't practice medicine. But, to save your life, I'll give you the psychic treatment if you'll agree as mayor not to push the license question.'

" 'Of course I will,' says he. 'And now get to work, Doc, for them pains are coming on again.'

" 'My fee will be $250.00, cure guaranteed in two treatments,' says I.

" 'All right,' says the Mayor. 'I'll pay it. I guess my life's worth that much.'

"I sat down by the bed and looked him straight in the eye.

" 'Now,' says I, 'get your mind off the disease. You ain't sick. You haven't got a heart or a clavicle or a funny bone or brains or anything. You haven't got any pain. Declare error. Now you feel the pain that you didn't have leaving, don't you?'

" 'I do feel some little better, Doc,' says the Mayor, 'darned if I don't. Now state a few lies about my not having this swelling in my left side, and I think I could be propped up and have some sausage and buckwheat cakes.'

"I made a few passes with my hands.

" 'Now,' says I, 'the inflammation's gone. The right lobe of the perihelion has subsided. You're getting sleepy. You can't hold your eyes open any longer. For the present the disease is checked. Now, you are asleep.'

"The Mayor shut his eyes slowly and began to snore.

" 'You observe, Mr. Tiddle,' says I, 'the wonders of modern science.'

" 'Biddle,' says he. 'When will you give uncle the rest of the treatment, Dr. Pooh-pooh?'

" 'Waugh-hoo,' says I. 'I'll come back at eleven to-morrow. When he wakes up give him eight drops of turpentine and three pounds of steak. Good morning.'

"The next morning I went back on time. 'Well, Mr. Riddle,' says I, when he opened the bedroom door, 'and how is uncle this morning?'

" 'He seems much better,' says the young man.

"The Mayor's color and pulse was fine. I gave him another treatment, and he said the last of the pain left him.

" 'Now,' says I, 'you'd better stay in bed for a day or two, and you'll be all right. It's a good thing I happened to be in Fisher Hill, Mr. Mayor,' says I, 'for all the remedies in the cornucopia that the regular schools of medicine use couldn't have saved you. And now that error has flew and pain proved a perjurer, let's allude to a cheerfuller subject — say the fee of $250. No checks, please, I hate to write my name on the back of a check almost as bad as I do on the front.'

" 'I've got the cash here,' says the Mayor, pulling a pocket book from under his pillow.

"He counts out five fifty-dollar notes and holds 'em in his hand.

" 'Bring the receipt,' he says to Biddle.

"I signed the receipt and the Mayor handed me the money. I put it in my inside pocket careful.

" 'Now do your duty, officer,' says the Mayor, grinning much unlike a sick man.

"Mr. Biddle lays his hand on my arm.

" 'You're under arrest, Dr. Waugh-hoo, alias Peters,' says he, 'for practising medicine without authority under the State law.'

" 'Who are you?' I asks.

" 'I'll tell you who he is,' says the Mayor, sitting up in bed. 'He's a detective employed by the State Medical Society. He's been following you over five counties. He came to me yesterday and we fixed up this scheme to catch you. I guess you won't do any more doctoring around these parts, Mr. Fakir. What was it you said I had, Doc?' the Mayor laughs, 'compound — well it wasn't softening of the brain, I guess, anyway.'

" 'A detective,' says I.

" 'Correct,' says Biddle. 'I'll have to turn you over to the sheriff.'

" 'Let's see you do it,' says I, and I grabs Biddle by the throat and half throws him out the window, but he pulls a gun and sticks it under my chin, and I stand still. Then he puts handcuffs on me, and takes the money out of my pocket.

" 'I witness,' says he, 'that they're the same bills that you and I marked, Judge Banks. I'll turn them over to the sheriff when we get to his office, and he'll send you a receipt. They'll have to be used as evidence in the case.'

" 'All right, Mr. Biddle,' says the Mayor. 'And now, Doc Waugh-hoo,' he goes on, 'why don't you demonstrate? Can't you pull the cork out of your magnetism with your teeth and hocus-pocus them hand-cuffs off?'

" 'Come on, officer,' says I, dignified. 'I may as well make the best of it.' And then I turns to old Banks and rattles my chains.

" 'Mr. Mayor,' says I, 'the time will come soon when you'll believe that personal magnetism is a success. And you'll be sure that it succeeded in this case, too.'

"And I guess it did.

"When we got nearly to the gate, I says: 'We might meet somebody now, Andy. I reckon you better take 'em off, and —' Hey? Why, of course it was Andy Tucker. That was his scheme; and that's how we got the capital to go into business together."

THE RANSOM OF RED CHIEF

IT looked like a good thing: but wait till I tell you. We were down South, in Alabama — Bill Driscoll and myself — when this kidnapping idea struck us. It was, as Bill afterward expressed it, "during a moment of temporary mental apparition"; but we didn't find that out till later.

There was a town down there, as flat as a flannel-cake, and called Summit, of course. It contained inhabitants of as undeleterious and self-satisfied a class of peasantry as ever clustered around a Maypole.

Bill and me had a joint capital of about six hundred dollars, and we needed just two thousand dollars more to pull off a fraudulent town-lot scheme in Western Illinois with. We talked it over on the front steps of the hotel. Philoprogenitiveness, says we, is strong in semi-rural communities; therefore, and for other reasons, a kidnapping project ought to do better there than in the radius of newspapers that send reporters out in plain clothes to stir up talk about such things. We knew that Summit couldn't get after us with anything stronger than constables and, maybe, some lackadaisical bloodhounds and a diatribe or two in the *Weekly Farmers' Budget.* So, it looked good.

We selected for our victim the only child of a prominent citizen named Ebenezer Dorset. The father was respectable and tight, a mortgage fancier and a stern, upright collection-plate passer and forecloser. The kid was a boy of ten, with bas-relief freckles, and hair the color of the cover of the magazine you buy at the news-stand when you want to catch a train. Bill and me figured that Ebenezer would melt down for a ransom of two thousand dollars to a cent. But wait till I tell you.

About two miles from Summit was a little mountain, covered with a dense cedar brake. On the rear elevation of this mountain was a cave. There we stored provisions.

One evening after sundown, we drove in a buggy past old Dorset's house. The kid was in the street, throwing rocks at a kitten on the opposite fence. "Hey, little boy!" says Bill, "would you like to have a bag of candy and a nice ride?"

The boy catches Bill neatly in the eye with a piece of brick.

"That will cost the old man an extra five hundred dollars," says Bill, climbing over the wheel.

That boy put up a fight like a welter-weight cinnamon bear; but, at last, we got him in the bottom of the buggy and drove away. We took him up to the cave, and I hitched the horse in the cedar brake. After dark I drove the buggy to the little village, three miles away, where we hired it, and walked back to the mountain.

Bill was pasting court-plaster over the scratches and bruises on his features. There was a fire burning behind the big rock at the entrance of the cave, and the boy was watching a pot of boiling coffee, with two buzzard tail-feathers stuck in his red hair. He points a stick at me when I come up, and says:

"Ha! cursed paleface, do you dare to enter the camp of Red Chief, the terror of the plains?"

"He's all right now," says Bill, rolling up his trousers and examining some bruises on his shins. "We're playing Indian. We're making Buffalo Bill's show look like magic-lantern views of Palestine in the town hall. I'm Old Hank, the Trapper, Red Chief's captive, and I'm to be scalped at daybreak. By Geronimo! that kid can kick hard."

Yes, sir, that boy seemed to be having the time of his life. The fun of camping out in a cave had made him forget that he was a captive himself. He immediately christened me Snake-eye, the Spy, and announced that, when his braves returned from the warpath, I was to be broiled at the stake at the rising of the sun.

Then we had supper; and he filled his mouth full of bacon and bread and gravy, and began to talk. He made a during-dinner speech something like this:

"I like this fine. I never camped out before; but I had a pet 'possum once, and I was nine last birthday. I hate to go to school. Rats ate up sixteen of Jimmy Talbot's aunt's speckled hen's eggs. Are there any real Indians in these woods? I want some more gravy. Does the trees moving make the wind blow? We had five puppies. What makes your nose so red, Hank? My father has lots of money. Are the stars hot? I whipped Ed Walker twice, Saturday. I don't like girls. You dassent catch toads unless with a string. Do oxen make any noise? Why are oranges round? Have you got beds to sleep on in this cave? Amos Murray has got six toes. A parrot can talk, but a monkey or a fish can't. How many does it take to make twelve?"

Every few minutes he would remember that he was a pesky redskin, and pick up his stick rifle and tiptoe to the mouth of the cave to rubber for the scouts of the hated paleface. Now and then he would let out a war-whoop that made Old Hank the Trapper shiver. That boy had Bill terrorized from the start.

"Red Chief," says I to the kid, "would you like to go home?"

"Aw, what for?" says he. "I don't have any fun at home. I hate to go to school. I like to camp out. You won't take me back home again, Snake-eye, will you?"

"Not right away," says I. "We'll stay here in the cave awhile."

"All right!" says he. "That'll be fine. I never had such fun in all my life."

We went to bed about eleven o'clock. We spread down some wide blankets and quilts and put Red Chief between us. We weren't afraid he'd run away. He kept us awake for three hours, jumping up and reaching for his rifle and screeching: "Hist! pard," in mine and Bill's ears, as the fancied crackle of a twig or the rustle of a leaf revealed to his young imagination the stealthy approach of the outlaw band. At last, I fell into a troubled sleep, and dreamed that I had been kidnapped and chained to a tree by a ferocious pirate with red hair.

Just at daybreak, I was awakened by a series of awful screams from Bill. They weren't yells, or howls, or shouts, or whoops, or yawps, such as you'd expect from a manly set of vocal organs — they were simply indecent, terrifying, humiliating screams, such as women emit when they see ghosts or caterpillars. It's an awful thing to hear a strong, desperate, fat man scream incontinently in a cave at daybreak.

I jumped up to see what the matter was. Red Chief was sitting on Bill's chest, with one hand twined in Bill's hair. In the other he had the sharp case-knife we used for slicing bacon; and he was industriously and realistically trying to take Bill's scalp, according to the sentence that had been pronounced upon him the evening before.

I got the knife away from the kid and made him lie down again. But, from that moment, Bill's spirit was broken. He laid down on his side of the bed, but he never closed an eye again in sleep as long as that boy was with us. I dozed off for a while, but along toward sun-up I remembered that Red Chief had said I was to be burned at the stake at the rising of the sun. I wasn't nervous or afraid; but I sat up and lit my pipe and leaned against a rock.

"What you getting up so soon for, Sam?" asked Bill.

"Me?" says I. "Oh, I got a kind of pain in my shoulder. I thought sitting up would rest it."

"You're a liar!" says Bill. "You're afraid. You was to be burned at sunrise, and you was afraid he'd do it. And he would, too, if he could find a match. Ain't it awful, Sam? Do you think anybody will pay out money to get a little imp like that back home?"

"Sure," said I. "A rowdy kid like that is just the kind that parents dote on. Now, you and the Chief get up and cook breakfast, while I go up on the top of this mountain and reconnoitre."

I went up on the peak of the little mountain and ran my eye over the contiguous vicinity. Over towards Summit I expected to see the sturdy yeomanry of the village armed with scythes and pitchforks beating the countryside for the dastardly kidnappers. But what I saw was a peaceful landscape dotted with one man ploughing with a dun mule. Nobody was dragging the creek; no couriers dashed hither and yon, bringing tidings of no news to the distracted parents. There was a sylvan attitude of somnolent sleepiness pervading that section of the external outward surface of Alabama that lay exposed to my view. "Perhaps," says I to myself, "it has not yet been discovered that the wolves have borne away the tender lambkin from the fold. Heaven help the wolves!" says I, and I went down the mountain to breakfast.

When I got to the cave I found Bill backed up against the side of it, breathing hard, and the boy threatening to smash him with a rock half as big as a cocoanut.

"He put a red-hot boiled potato down my back," explained Bill, "and then mashed it with his foot; and I boxed his ears. Have you got a gun about you, Sam?"

I took the rock away from the boy and kind of patched up the argument. "I'll fix you," says the kid to Bill. "No man ever yet struck Red Chief but he got paid for it. You better beware!"

After breakfast the kid takes a piece of leather with strings wrapped around it out of his pocket and goes outside the cave unwinding it.

"What's he up to now?" says Bill, anxiously. "You don't think he'll run away, do you, Sam?"

"No fear of it," says I. "He don't seem to be much of a home body. But we've got to fix up some plan about the ransom. There don't seem to be much excitement around Summit on account of his disappearance; but maybe they haven't realized yet that he's gone. His folks may think he's spending the night with Aunt Jane or one of the neighbors. Anyhow, he'll be missed to-day. To-night we must get a message to his father demanding two thousand dollars for his return."

Just then we heard a kind of war-whoop, such as David might have emitted when he knocked out the champion Goliath. It was a sling that Red Chief had pulled out of his pocket, and he was whirling it around his head.

I dodged, and heard a heavy thud and a kind of a sigh from Bill, like a horse gives out when you take his saddle off. A rounded off rock the size of an egg had caught Bill just behind his left ear. He loosened himself all over and fell in the fire across the frying pan of hot water for washing dishes. I dragged him out and poured cold water on his head.

By and by, Bill sits up and feels behind his ear and says: "Sam, do you know who my favorite Biblical character is?"

"Take it easy," says I. "You'll come to your senses presently."

"King Herod," says he. "You won't go away and leave me here alone, will you, Sam?"

I went out and caught that boy and shook him until his freckles rattled. "If you don't behave," says I, "I'll take you straight home. Now, are you going to be good, or not?"

"I was only funning," says he, sullenly. "I didn't mean to hurt Old Hank. But what did he hit me for? I'll behave, Snake-eye, if you won't send me home, and if you'll let me play the Black Scout to-day."

"I don't know the game," says I. "That's for you and Mr. Bill to decide. He's your playmate for the day. I'm going away for a while, on business. Now, you come in and make friends with him and say you are sorry for hurting him, or home you go, at once."

I made him and Bill shake hands, and then I took Bill aside and told him I was going to Poplar Cove, a little village three miles from the cave, and find out what I could about how the kidnapping had been regarded in Summit. Also, I thought it best to send a peremptory letter to old man Dorset that day, demanding the ransom and dictating how it should be paid.

"You know, Sam," says Bill, "I've stood by you without batting an eye in earthquakes, fire and flood — in poker games, dynamite outrages, police raids, train robberies, and cyclones. I never lost my nerve yet till we kidnapped that two-legged skyrocket of a kid. He's got me going. You won't leave me long with him, will you, Sam?"

"I'll be back some time this afternoon," says I. "You must keep the boy amused and quiet till I return. And now we'll write the letter to old Dorset."

Bill and I got paper and pencil and worked on the letter while Red Chief, with a blanket wrapped around him, strutted up and down, guarding the mouth of the cave. Bill begged me tearfully to make the ransom fifteen hundred dollars instead of two thousand. "I ain't attempting," says he, "to decry the celebrated moral aspect of parental affection, but we're dealing with humans, and it ain't human for anybody to give up two thousand dollars for that forty-pound chunk of freckled wildcat. I'm willing to take a chance at fifteen hundred dollars. You can charge the difference up to me." So, to relieve Bill, I acceded, and we collaborated a letter that ran this way:

EBENEZER DORSET, ESQ.:

We have your boy concealed in a place far from Summit. It is use-
less for you or the most skilful detectives to attempt to find him. Abso-
lutely, the only terms on which you can have him restored to you are
these: We demand fifteen hundred dollars in large bills for his return;
the money to be left at midnight to-night at the same spot and in the
same box as your reply — as hereinafter described. If you agree to these
terms, send your answer in writing by a solitary messenger to-night at
half-past eight o'clock. After crossing Owl Creek on the road to Poplar
Grove, there are three large trees about a hundred yards apart, close
to the fence of the wheat field on the right-hand side. At the bottom of
the fence-post, opposite the third tree, will be found a small pasteboard box.

The messenger will place the answer in this box and return immediately to Summit.

If you attempt any treachery, or fail to comply with our demand as
stated, you will never see your boy again.

If you pay the money as demanded, he will be returned to you safe
and well within three hours. These terms are final, and if you do not
accede to them no further communications will be attempted.

TWO DESPERATE MEN.

I addressed this letter to Dorset, and put it in my pocket. As I was
about to start, the kid comes up to me and says:

"Aw, Snake-eye, you said I could play the Black Scout while you
was gone."

"Play it, of course," says I. "Mr. Bill will play with you. What kind
of a game is it?"

"I'm the Black Scout," says Red Chief, "and I have to ride to the
stockade to warn the settlers that the Indians are coming. I'm tired of
playing Indian myself. I want to be the Black Scout."

"All right," says I. "It sounds harmless to me. I guess Mr. Bill will
help you foil the pesky savages."

"What am I to do?" asks Bill, looking at the kid suspiciously.

"You are the hoss," says Black Scout. "Get down on your hands and
knees. How can I ride to the stockade without a hoss?"

"You'd better keep him interested," said I, "till we get the scheme
going. Loosen up."

Bill gets down on all fours, and a look comes in his eye like a
rabbit's when you catch it in a trap.

"How far is it to the stockade, kid?" he asks, in a husky voice.

"Ninety miles," says the Black Scout. "And you have to hump yourself to get there on time. Whoa, now!"

The Black Scout jumps on Bill's back and digs his heels in his side.

"For heaven's sake," says Bill, "hurry back, Sam, as soon as you can. I wish we hadn't made the ransom more than a thousand. Say, you quit kicking me or I'll get up and warm you good."

I walked over to Poplar Cove and sat around the post-office and store, talking with the chaw-bacons that came in to trade. One whis-kerando says that he hears Summit is all upset on account of Elder Ebenezer Dorset's boy having been lost or stolen. That was all I wanted to know. I bought some smoking tobacco, referred casually to the price of blackeyed peas, posted my letter surreptitiously, and came away. The postmaster said the mail-carrier would come by in an hour to take the mail on to Summit.

When I got back to the cave Bill and the boy were not to be found. I explored the vicinity of the cave, and risked a yodel or two, but there was no response.

So I lighted my pipe and sat down on a mossy bank to await develop-ments.

In about half an hour I heard the bushes rustle, and Bill wabbled out into the little glade in front of the cave. Behind him was the kid, step-ping softly like a scout, with a broad grin on his face. Bill stopped, took off his hat, and wiped his face with a red handerkerchief. The kid stopped about eight feet behind him.

"Sam," says Bill, "I suppose you'll think I'm a renegade, but I couldn't help it. I'm a grown person with masculine proclivities and habits of self-defense, but there is a time when all systems of egotism and predominance fail. The boy is gone. I sent him home. All is off. There was martyrs in old times," goes on Bill, "that suffered death rather than give up the particular graft they enjoyed. None of 'em ever was subjugated to such supernatural tortures as I have been. I tried to be faithful to our articles of depredation; but there came a limit."

"What's the trouble, Bill?" I asks him.

"I was rode," says Bill, "the ninety miles to the stockade, not bar-ring an inch. Then, when the settlers was rescued, I was given oats. Sand ain't a palatable substitute. And then, for an hour I had to try to explain to him why there was nothin' in holes, how a road can run both ways, and what makes the grass green. I tell you, Sam, a human can only stand so much. I takes him by the neck of his clothes and drags him down the mountain. On the way he kicks my legs black and blue from the knees down; and I've got to have two or three bites on my thumb and hand cauterized.

"But he's gone" — continues Bill — "gone home. I showed him the road to Summit and kicked him about eight feet nearer there at one kick. I'm sorry we lose the ransom; but it was either that or Bill Driscoll to the madhouse."

Bill is puffing and blowing, but there is a look of ineffable peace and growing content on his rose-pink features.

"Bill," says I, "there isn't any heart disease in your family, is there?"

"No," says Bill, "nothing chronic except malaria and accidents. Why?"

"Then you might turn around," says I, "and have a look behind you."

Bill turns and sees the boy, and loses his complexion and sits down plump on the ground and begins to pluck aimlessly at grass and little sticks. For an hour I was afraid of his mind. And then I told him that my scheme was to put the whole job through immediately and that we would get the ransom and be off with it by midnight if old Dorset fell in with our proposition. So Bill braced up enough to give the kid a weak sort of a smile and a promise to play the Russian in a Japanese war with him as soon as he felt a li tle better.

I had a scheme for collecting that ransom without danger of being caught by counterplots that ought to commend itself to professional kidnappers. The tree under which the answer was to be left — and the money later on — was close to the road fence with big, bare fields on all sides. If a gang of constables should be watching for any one to come for the note they could see him a long way off crossing the fields or in the road. But no, sirree! At half-past eight I was up in that tree as well hidden as a tree toad, waiting for the messenger to arrive.

Exactly on time, a half-grown boy rides up the road on a bicycle, locates the pasteboard box at the foot of the fence-post, slips a folded piece of paper into it, and pedals away again back toward Summit.

I waited an hour and then concluded the thing was square. I slid down the tree, got the note, slipped along the fence till I struck the woods, and was back at the cave in another half an hour. I opened the note, got near the lantern, and read it to Bill. It was written with a pen in a crabbed hand, and the sum and substance of it was this:

Two Desperate Men.

Gentlemen: I received your letter to-day by post, in regard to the ransom you ask for the return of my son. I think you are a little high in your demands, and I hereby make you a counter-proposition, which I am inclined to believe you will accept. You bring Johnny home and pay me two hundred and fifty dollars in cash, and I agree to take him off your hands. You had better come at night, for the neighbors believe he is lost, and I couldn't be responsible for what they would do to anybody they saw bringing him back. Very respectfully,

EBENEZER DORSET.

"Great pirates of Penzance," says I; "of all the impudent —"

But I glanced at Bill, and hesitated. He had the most appealing look in his eyes I ever saw on the face of a dumb or a talking brute.

"Sam," says he, "what's two hundred and fifty dollars, after all? We've got the money. One more night of this kid will send me to a bed in Bedlam. Besides being a thorough gentleman, I think Mr. Dorset is a spendthrift for making us such a liberal offer. You ain't going to let the chance go, are you?"

"Tell you the truth, Bill," says I, "this little ewe lamb has somewhat got on my nerves too. We'll take him home, pay the ransom, and make our getaway."

We took him home that night. We got him to go by telling him that his father had bought a silver-mounted rifle and a pair of moccasins for him, and we were to hunt bears the next day.

It was just twelve o'clock when we knocked at Ebenezer's front door. Just at the moment when I should have been abstracting the fifteen hundred dollars from the box under the tree, according to the original proposition, Bill was counting out two hundred and fifty dollars into Dorset's hand.

When the kid found out we were going to leave him at home he started up a howl like a calliope and fastened himself as tight as a leech to Bill's leg. His father peeled him away gradually, like a porous plaster.

"How long can you hold him?" asks Bill.

"I'm not as strong as I used to be," says old Dorset, "but I think I can promise you ten minutes."

"Enough," says Bill. "In ten minutes I shall cross the Central, Southern, and Middle Western States, and be legging it trippingly for the Canadian border."

And, as dark as it was, and as fat as Bill was, and as good a runner as I am, he was a good mile and a half out of Summit before I could catch up with him.

A RETRIEVED REFORMATION

A GUARD came to the prison shoe-shop, where Jimmy Valentine was assiduously stitching uppers, and escorted him to the front office. There the warden handed Jimmy his pardon, which had been signed that morning by the governor. Jimmy took it in a tired kind of way. He had served nearly ten months of a four-year sentence. He had expected to stay only about three months, at the longest. When a man with as many friends on the outside as Jimmy Valentine had is received in the "stir" it is hardly worth while to cut his hair.

"Now, Valentine," said the warden, "you'll go out in the morning. Brace up, and make a man of yourself. You're not a bad fellow at heart. Stop cracking safes, and live straight."

"Me?" said Jimmy, in surprise. "Why, I never cracked a safe in my life."

"Oh, no," laughed the warden. "Of course not. Let's see, now. How was it you happened to get sent up on that Springfield job? Was it because you wouldn't prove an alibi for fear of compromising somebody in extremely high-toned society? Or was it simply a case of a mean old jury that had it in for you? It's always one or the other with you innocent victims."

"Me?" said Jimmy, still blankly virtuous. "Why, warden, I never was in Springfield in my life!"

"Take him back, Cronin," smiled the warden, "and fix him up with outgoing clothes. Unlock him at seven in the morning, and let him come to the bull-pen. Better think over my advice, Valentine."

At a quarter past seven on the next morning Jimmy stood in the warden's outer office. He had on a suit of the villainously fitting, ready-made clothes and a pair of the stiff, squeaky shoes that the state furnishes to its discharged compulsory guests.

The clerk handed him a railroad ticket and the five-dollar bill with which the law expected him to rehabilitate himself into good citizenship and prosperity. The warden gave him a cigar, and shook hands. Valentine, 9762, was chronicled on the books "Pardoned by Governor," and Mr. James Valentine walked out into the sunshine.

Disregarding the song of the birds, the waving green trees, and the smell of the flowers, Jimmy headed straight for a restaurant. There he tasted the first sweet joys of liberty in the shape of a broiled chicken and a bottle of white wine — followed by a cigar a grade better than

the one the warden had given him. From there he proceeded lei-
surely to the depot. He tossed a quarter into the hat of a blind man
sitting by the door, and boarded his train. Three hours set him down
in a little town near the state line. He went to the café of one Mike
Dolan and shook hands with Mike, who was alone behind the bar.

"Sorry we couldn't make it sooner, Jimmy, me boy," said Mike.
"But we had that protest from Springfield to buck against, and the
governor nearly balked. Feeling all right?"

"Fine," said Jimmy. "Got my key?"

He got his key and went upstairs, unlocking the door of a room at
the rear. Everything was just as he had left it. There on the floor was
still Ben Price's collar-button that had been torn from that eminent
detective's shirt-band when they had overpowered Jimmy to arrest
him.

Pulling out from the wall a folding-bed, Jimmy slid back a panel
in the wall and dragged out a dust-covered suit-case. He opened this
and gazed fondly at the finest set of burglar's tools in the East. It was
a complete set, made of specially tempered steel, the latest designs in
drills, punches, braces and bits, jimmies, clamps, and augers, with
two or three novelties invented by Jimmy himself, in which he took
pride. Over nine hundred dollars they had cost him to have made
at —, a place where they make such things for the profession.

In half an hour Jimmy went downstairs and through the café. He
was now dressed in tasteful and well-fitting clothes, and carried his
dusted and cleaned suitcase in his hand.

"Got anything on?" asked Mike Dolan, genially.

"Me?" said Jimmy, in a puzzled tone. "I don't understand. I'm
representing the New York Amalgamated Short Snap Biscuit Cracker
and Frazzled Wheat Company."

This statement delighted Mike to such an extent that Jimmy had
to take a seltzer-and-milk on the spot. He never touched "hard"
drinks.

A week after the release of Valentine, 9762, there was a neat job of
safe-burglary done in Richmond, Indiana, with no clue to the author.
A scant eight hundred dollars was all that was secured. Two weeks
after that a patented, improved, burglar-proof safe in Logansport was
opened like a cheese to the tune of fifteen hundred dollars, currency;
securities and silver untouched. That began to interest the rogue-
catchers. Then an old-fashioned bank-safe in Jefferson City became
active and threw out of its crater an eruption of bank-notes amounting to five thousand dollars. The losses were now high enough to

bring the matter up into Ben Price's class of work. By comparing notes, a remarkable similarity in the methods of the burglaries was noticed. Ben Price investigated the scenes of the robberies, and was heard to remark:

"That's Dandy Jim Valentine's autograph. He's resumed business. Look at that combination knob — jerked out as easy as pulling up a radish in wet weather. He's got the only clamps that can do it. And look how clean those tumblers were punched out! Jimmy never has to drill but one hole. Yes, I guess I want Mr. Valentine. He'll do his bit next time without any short-time or clemency foolishness."

Ben Price knew Jimmy's habits. He had learned them while working up the Springfield case. Long jumps, quick get-aways, no confederates, and a taste for good society — these ways had helped Mr. Valentine to become noted as a successful dodger of retribution. It was given out that Ben Price had taken up the trail of the elusive cracksman, and other people with burglar-proof safes felt more at ease.

One afternoon Jimmy Valentine and his suit-case climbed out of the mailhack in Elmore, a little town five miles off the railroad down in the black-jack country of Arkansas. Jimmy, looking like an athletic young senior just home from college, went down the broad sidewalk toward the hotel.

A young lady crossed the street, passed him at the corner and entered a door over which was the sign "The Elmore Bank." Jimmy Valentine looked into her eyes, forgot what he was, and became another man. She lowered her eyes and colored slightly. Young men of Jimmy's style and looks were scarce in Elmore.

Jimmy collared a boy that was loafing on the steps of the bank as if he were one of the stock-holders, and began to ask him questions about the town, feeding him dimes at intervals. By and by the young lady came out, looking royally unconscious of the young man with the suitcase, and went her way.

"Isn't that young lady Miss Polly Simpson?" asked Jimmy, with specious guile.

"Naw," said the boy. "She's Annabel Adams. Her pa owns this bank. What'd you come to Elmore for? Is that a gold watch-chain? I'm going to get a bulldog. Got any more dimes?"

Jimmy went to the Planters' Hotel, registered as Ralph D. Spencer, and engaged a room. He leaned on the desk and declared his platform to the clerk. He said he had come to Elmore to look for a location to go into business. How was the shoe business, now, in the town? He had thought of the shoe business. Was there an opening?

The clerk was impressed by the clothes and manner of Jimmy. He, himself, was something of a pattern of fashion to the thinly gilded youth of Elmore, but he now perceived his shortcomings. While trying to figure out Jimmy's manner of tying his four-in-hand he cordially gave information.

Yes, there ought to be a good opening in the shoe line. There wasn't an exclusive shoe-store in the place. The dry-goods and general stores handled them. Business in all lines was fairly good. Hoped Mr. Spencer would decide to locate in Elmore. He would find it a pleasant town to live in, and the people very sociable.

Mr. Spencer thought he would stop over in the town a few days and look over the situation. No, the clerk needn't call the boy. He would carry up his suitcase himself; it was rather heavy.

Mr. Ralph Spencer, the phœnix that arose from Jimmy Valentine's ashes — ashes left by the flame of a sudden and alterative attack of love — remained in Elmore, and prospered. He opened a shoe-store and secured a good run of trade.

Socially he was also a success, and made many friends. And he accomplished the wish of his heart. He met Miss Annabel Adams, and became more and more captivated by her charms.

At the end of a year the situation of Mr. Ralph Spencer was this: he had won the respect of the community, his shoe-store was flourishing, and he and Annabel were engaged to be married in two weeks. Mr. Adams, the typical, plodding, country banker, approved of Spencer. Annabel's pride in him almost equalled her affection. He was as much at home in the family of Mr. Adams and that of Annabel's married sister as if he were already a member.

One day Jimmy sat down in his room and wrote this letter, which he mailed to the safe address of one of his old friends in St. Louis:

Dear Old Pal:

I want you to be at Sullivan's place, in Little Rock, next Wednesday night, at nine o'clock. I want you to wind up some little matters for me. And, also, I want to make you a present of my kit of tools. I know you'll be glad to get them — you couldn't duplicate the lot for a thousand dollars. Say, Billy, I've quit the old business — a year ago. I've got a nice store. I'm making an honest living, and I'm going to marry the finest girl on earth two weeks from now. It's the only life, Billy — the straight one. I wouldn't touch a dollar of another man's money now for a million. After I get married I'm going to sell out and go West, where there won't be so much danger of having old scores brought up against me. I tell you, Billy, she's an angel. She believes in me; and I wouldn't do another crooked thing for the whole world. Be sure to be at Sully's, for I must see you. I'll bring along the tools with me.

Your old friend,
JIMMY.

On the Monday night after Jimmy wrote this letter, Ben Price jogged unobtrusively into Elmore in a livery buggy. He lounged about town in his quiet way until he found out what he wanted to know. From the drug-store across the street from Spencer's shoe-store he got a good look at Ralph D. Spencer.

"Going to marry the banker's daughter are you, Jimmy?" said Ben to himself, softly. "Well, I don't know!"

The next morning Jimmy took breakfast at the Adamses. He was going to Little Rock that day to order his wedding-suit and buy something nice for Annabel. That would be the first time he had left town since he came to Elmore. It had been more than a year now since those last professional "jobs," and he thought he could safely venture out.

After breakfast quite a family party went down town together — Mr. Adams, Annabel, Jimmy, and Annabel's married sister with her two little girls, aged five and nine. They came by the hotel where Jimmy still boarded, and he ran up to his room and brought along his suitcase. Then they went on to the bank. There stood Jimmy's horse and buggy and Dolph Gibson, who was going to drive him over to the railroad station.

All went inside the high, carved oak railings into the banking-room — Jimmy included, for Mr. Adams's future son-in-law was welcome anywhere. The clerks were pleased to be greeted by the good-looking, agreeable young man who was going to marry Miss Annabel. Jimmy set his suit-case down. Annabel, whose heart was bubbling with happiness and lively youth, put on Jimmy's hat and picked up the suit-case. "Wouldn't I make a nice drummer?" said Annabel. "My, Ralph, how heavy it is. Feels like it was full of gold bricks."

"Lot of nickel-plated shoe-horns in there," said Jimmy, coolly, "that I'm going to return. Thought I'd save express charges by taking them up. I'm getting awfully economical."

The Elmore Bank had just put in a new safe and vault. Mr. Adams was very proud of it, and insisted on an inspection by every one. The vault was a small one, but it had a new patented door. It fastened with three solid steel bolts thrown simultaneously with a single handle, and had a time-lock. Mr. Adams beamingly explained its workings to Mr. Spencer, who showed a courteous but not too intelligent interest. The two children, May and Agatha, were delighted by the shining metal and funny clock and knobs.

While they were thus engaged Ben Price sauntered in and leaned on his elbow, looking casually inside between the railings. He told the teller that he didn't want anything; he was just waiting for a man he knew.

Suddenly there was a scream or two from the women, and a commotion. Unperceived by the elders, May, the nine-year-old girl, in a spirit of play, had shut Agatha in the vault. She had then shot the bolts and turned the knob of the combination as she had seen Mr. Adams do.

The old banker sprang to the handle and tugged at it for a moment. "The door can't be opened," he groaned. "The clock hasn't been wound nor the combination set."

Agatha's mother screamed again, hysterically.

"Hush!" said Mr. Adams, raising his trembling hand. "All be quiet for a moment. Agatha!" he called as loudly as he could. "Listen to me." During the following silence they could just hear the faint sound of the child wildly shrieking in the dark vault in a panic of terror.

"My precious darling!" wailed the mother. "She will die of fright! Open the door! Oh, break it open! Can't you men do something?"

"There isn't a man nearer than Little Rock who can open that door," said Mr. Adams, in a shaky voice. "My God! Spencer, what shall we do? That child — she can't stand it long in there. There isn't enough air, and, besides, she'll go into convulsions from fright."

Agatha's mother, frantic now, beat the door of the vault with her hands. Somebody wildly suggested dynamite. Annabel turned to Jimmy, her large eyes full of anguish, but not yet despairing. To a woman nothing seems quite impossible to the powers of the man she worships.

"Can't you do something, Ralph — *try,* won't you?"

He looked at her with a queer, soft smile on his lips and in his keen eyes.

"Annabel," he said, "give me that rose you are wearing, will you?"

Hardly believing that she heard him aright, she unpinned the bud from the bosom of her dress, and placed it in his hand. Jimmy stuffed it into his vestpocket, threw off his coat and pulled up his shirt-sleeves.

With that act Ralph D. Spencer passed away and Jimmy Valentine took his place.

"Get way from the door, all of you," he commanded, shortly.

He set his suit-case on the table, and opened it out flat. From that time on he seemed to be unconscious of the presence of any one else. He laid out the shining, queer implements swiftly and orderly, whistling softly to himself as he always did when at work. In a deep silence and immovable, the others watched him as if under a spell.

In a minute Jimmy's pet drill was biting smoothly into the steel door. In ten minutes — breaking his own burglarious record — he threw back the bolts and opened the door.

Agatha, almost collapsed, but safe, was gathered into her mother's arms.

Jimmy Valentine put on his coat, and walked outside the railings toward the front door. As he went he thought he heard a far-away voice that he once knew call "Ralph!" But he never hesitated.

At the door a big man stood somewhat in his way.

"Hello, Ben!" said Jimmy, still with his strange smile. "Got around at last, have you? Well, let's go. I don't know that it makes much difference, now."

And then Ben Price acted rather strangely.

"Guess you're mistaken, Mr. Spencer," he said. "Don't believe I recognize you. Your buggy's waiting for you, ain't it?"

And Ben Price turned and strolled down the street.

BABES IN THE JUNGLE

Montague Silver, the finest street man and art grafter in the West, says to me once in Little Rock: "If you ever lose your mind, Billy, and get too old to do honest swindling among grown men, go to New York. In the West a sucker is born every minute; but in New York they appear in chunks of roe — you can't count 'em!"

Two years afterwards I found that I couldn't remember the names of the Russian admirals, and I noticed some gray hairs over my left ear; so I knew the time had arrived for me to take Silver's advice.

I struck New York about noon one day, and took a walk up Broadway. And I run against Silver himself, all encompassed up in a spacious kind of haberdashery, leaning against a hotel and rubbing the half-moons on his nails with a silk handkerchief.

"Paresis or superannuated?" I asks him.

"Hello, Billy," says Silver; "I'm glad to see you. Yes, it seemed to me that the West was accumulating a little too much wiseness. I've been saving New York for dessert. I know it's a low-down trick to take things from these people. They only know this and that and pass to fro and think ever and anon. I'd hate for my mother to know I was skinning these weak-minded ones. She raised me better."

"Is there a crush already in the waiting rooms of the old doctor that does skin grafting?" I asks.

"Well, no," says Silver; "you needn't back Epidermis to win today. I've only been here a month. But I'm ready to begin; and the members of Willie Manhattan's Sunday School class, each of whom has volunteered to contribute a portion of cuticle toward this rehabilitation, may as well send their photos to the *Evening Daily*.

"I've been studying the town," says Silver, "and reading the papers every day, and I know it as well as the cat in the City Hall knows an O'Sullivan. People here lie down on the floor and scream and kick when you are the least bit slow about taking money from them. Come up in my room and I'll tell you. We'll work the town together, Billy, for the sake of old times."

Silver takes me up in a hotel. He has a quantity of irrelevant objects lying about.

"There's more ways of getting money from these metropolitan hay-seeds," says Silver, "than there is of cooking rice in Charleston, S. C. They'll bite at anything. The brains of most of 'em commute. The wiser they are in intelligence the less perception of cognizance they have. Why, didn't a man the other day sell J. P. Morgan an oil portrait of Rockefeller, Jr., for Andrea del Sarto's celebrated painting of the young Saint John!

"You see that bundle of printed stuff in the corner, Billy? That's gold mining stock. I started out one day to sell that, but I quit it in two hours. Why? Got arrested for blocking the street. People fought to buy it. I sold the policeman a block of it on the way to the station-house, and then I took it off the market. I don't want people to give me their money. I want some little consideration connected with the transaction to keep my pride from being hurt. I want 'em to guess the missing letter in Chic—go, or draw to a pair of nines before they pay me a cent of money.

"Now there's another little scheme that worked so easy I had to quit it. You see that bottle of blue ink on the table? I tattooed an anchor on the back of my hand and went to a bank and told 'em I was Admiral Dewey's nephew. They offered to cash my draft on him for a thousand, but I didn't know my uncle's first name. It shows, though, what an easy town it is. As for burglars, they won't go in a house now unless there's a hot supper ready and a few college students to wait on 'em. They're slugging citizens all over the upper part of the city and I guess, taking the town from end to end, it's a plain case of assault and Battery."

"Monty," says I, when Silver had slacked up, "you may have Manhattan correctly discriminated in your perorative, but I doubt it. I've only been in town two hours, but it don't dawn upon me that it's ours with a cherry in it. There ain't enough rus in urbe about it to suit me. I'd be a good deal much better satisfied if the citizens had a straw or more in their hair, and run more to velveteen vests and buckeye watch charms. They don't look easy to me."

"You've got it, Billy," says Silver. "All emigrants have it. New York's bigger than Little Rock or Europe, and it frightens a foreigner. You'll be all right. I tell you I feel like slapping the people here because they don't send me all their money in laundry baskets, with germicide sprinkled over it. I hate to go down on the street to get it. Who wears the diamonds in this town? Why, Winnie, the Wiretapper's wife, and Bella, the Buncosteerer's bride. New Yorkers can be worked easier than a blue rose on a tidy. The only thing that bothers me is I know I'll break the cigars in my vest pocket when I get my clothes all full of twenties."

"I hope you are right, Monty," says I; "but I wish all the same I had

been satisfied with a small business in Little Rock. The crop of farmers is never so short out there but what you can get a few of 'em to
sign a petition for a new post office that you can discount for $200 at
the county bank. The people here appear to possess instincts of self-
preservation and illiberality. I fear me that we are not cultivated
enough to tackle this game."

"Don't worry," says Silver. "I've got this Jayville-Tarrytown correctly estimated as sure as North River is the Hudson and East river
ain't a river. Why, there are people living in four blocks of Broadway
who never saw any kind of a building except a skyscraper in their
lives! A good, live hustling Western man ought to get conspicuous
enough here inside of three months to incur either Jerome's clemency
or Lawson's displeasure."

"Hyperbole aside," says I, "do you know of any immediate system
of buncoing the community out of a dollar or two except by applying
to the Salvation Army or having a fit on Miss Helen Gould's door-
steps?"

"Dozens of 'em," says Silver. "How much capital have you got,
Billy?"

"A thousand." I told him.

"I've got $1,200," says he. "We'll pool and do a big business. There's
so many ways we can make a million that I don't know how to begin."

The next morning Silver meets me at the hotel and he is all sonorous and stirred with a kind of silent joy.

"We're to meet J. P. Morgan this afternoon," says he. "A man I
know in the hotel wants to introduce us. He's a friend of his. He says
he likes to meet people from the West."

"That sounds nice and plausible," says I. "I'd like to know Mr.
Morgan."

"It won't hurt us a bit," says Silver, "to get acquainted with a few
finance kings. I kind of like the social way New York has with
strangers."

The man Silver knew was named Klein. At three o'clock Klein
brought his Wall Street friend to see us in Silver's room. "Mr. Morgan" looked some like his pictures, and he had a Turkish towel
wrapped around his left foot, and he walked with a cane.

"Mr. Silver and Mr. Pescud," says Klein. "It sounds superfluous,"
says he, "to mention the name of the greatest financial —"

"Cut it out, Klein," says Mr. Morgan. "I'm glad to know you gents;
I take great interest in the West. Klein tells me you're from Little
Rock. I think I've a railroad or two out there somewhere. If either

of you guys would like to deal a hand or two of stud poker I —"

"Now, Pierpont," cuts in Klein, "you forget!"

"Excuse me, gents!" says Morgan; "since I've had the gout so bad I sometimes play a social game of cards at my house. Neither of you never knew One-eyed Peters, did you, while you was around Little Rock? He lived in Seattle, New Mexico."

Before we could answer, Mr. Morgan hammered on the floor with his cane and begins to walk up and down, swearing in a loud tone of voice.

"They have been pounding your stocks to-day on the Street, Pierpont?" asks Klein, smiling.

"Stocks! No!" roars Mr. Morgan. "It's that picture I sent an agent to Europe to buy. I just thought about it. He cabled me to-day that it ain't to be found in all Italy. I'd pay $50,000 to-morrow for that picture — yes, $75,000. I give the agent a la carte in purchasing it. I cannot understand why the art galleries will allow a De Vinchy to —"

"Why, Mr. Morgan," says Klein; "I thought you owned all of the De Vinchy paintings."

'What is the picture like, Mr. Morgan?" asks Silver. "It must be as big as the side of the Flatiron Building."

"I'm afraid your art education is on the bum, Mr. Silver," says Morgan. "The picture is 27 inches by 42; and it is called 'Love's Idle Hour.' It represents a number of cloak models doing the two-step on the bank of a purple river. The cablegram said it might have been brought to this country. My collection will never be complete without that picture. Well, so long, gents; us financiers must keep early hours."

Mr. Morgan and Klein went away together in a cab. Me and Silver talked about how simple and unsuspecting great people was; and Silver said what a shame it would be to try to rob a man like Mr. Morgan; and I said I thought it would be rather imprudent, myself. Klein proposes a stroll after dinner; and me and him and Silver walks down toward Seventh Avenue to see the sights. Klein sees a pair of cuff links that instigate his admiration in a pawnshop window, and we all go in while he buys 'em.

After we got back to the hotel and Klein had gone, Silver jumps at me and waves his hands.

"Did you see it?" says he. "Did you see it, Billy?"

"What?" I asks.

"Why, that picture that Morgan wants. It's hanging in the pawnshop, behind the desk. I didn't say anything because Klein was there.

It's the article sure as you live. The girls are as natural as paint can make them, all measuring 36 and 25 and 42 skirts, if they had any skirts, and they're doing a buck-and-wing on the bank of a river with the blues. What did Mr. Morgan say he'd give for it? Oh, don't make me tell you. They can't know what it is in that pawnshop."

When the pawnshop opened the next morning me and Silver was standing there as anxious as if we wanted to soak our Sunday suit to buy a drink. We sauntered inside, and began to look at watch-chains.

"That's a violent specimen of a chromo you've got up there," remarked Silver, casual, to the pawnbroker. "But I kind of enthuse over the girl with the shoulder-blades and red bunting. Would an offer of $2.25 for it cause you to knock over any fragile articles of your stock in hurrying it off the nail?"

The pawnbroker smiles and goes on showing us plate watch-chains.

"That picture," says he, "was pledged a year ago by an Italian gentleman. I loaned him $500 on it. It is called 'Love's Idle Hour,' and it is by Leonardo de Vinchy. Two days ago the legal time expired, and it became an unredeemed pledge. Here is a style of chain that is worn a great deal now."

At the end of half an hour me and Silver paid the pawnbroker $2,000 and walked out with the picture. Silver got into a cab with it and started for Morgan's office. I goes to the hotel and waits for him. In two hours Silver comes back.

"Did you see Mr. Morgan?" I asks. "How much did he pay you for it?"

Silver sits down and fools with a tassel on the table cover.

"I never exactly saw Mr. Morgan," he says, "because Mr. Morgan's been in Europe for a month. But what's worrying me, Billy, is this: The department stores have all got that same picture on sale, framed, for $3.48. And they charge $3.50 for the frame alone — that's what I can't understand."

A DOUBLE-DYED DECEIVER

THE trouble began in Laredo. It was the Llano Kid's fault, for he should have confined his habit of manslaughter to Mexicans. But the Kid was past twenty; and to have only Mexicans to one's credit at twenty is to blush unseen on the Rio Grande border.

It happened in old Justo Valdo's gambling house. There was a poker game at which sat players who were not all friends, as happens often where men ride in from afar to shoot Folly as she gallops. There was a row over so small a matter as a pair of queens; and when the smoke had cleared away it was found that the Kid had committed an indiscretion, and his adversary had been guilty of a blunder. For, the unfortunate combatant, instead of being a Mexican was a high-blooded youth from the cow ranches, of about the Kid's own age and possessed of friends and champions. His blunder in missing the Kid's right ear only a sixteenth of an inch when he pulled his gun did not lessen the indiscretion of the better marksman.

The Kid, not being equipped with a retinue, nor bountifully supplied with personal admirers and supporters — on account of a rather umbrageous reputation, even for the border — considered it not incompatible with his indisputable gameness to perform that judicious tractional act known as "pulling his freight."

Quickly the avengers gathered and sought him. Three of them overtook him within a rod of the station. The Kid turned and showed his teeth in that brilliant but mirthless smile that usually preceded his deeds of insolence and violence, and his pursuers fell back without making it necessary for him even to reach for his weapon.

But in this affair the Kid had not felt the grim thirst for encounter that usually urged him on to battle. It had been a purely chance row, born of the cards and certain epithets impossible for a gentleman to brook that had passed between the two. The Kid had rather liked the slim, haughty, brown-faced young chap whom his bullet had cut off in the first pride of manhood. And now he wanted no more blood. He wanted to get away and have a good long sleep somewhere in the sun on the mesquite grass with his handkerchief over his face. Even a Mexican might have crossed his path in safety while he was in this mood.

The Kid openly boarded the north-bound passenger train that departed five minutes later. But at Webb, a few miles out, where it was

75

flagged to take on a traveller, he abandoned that manner of escape. There were telegraph stations ahead; and the Kid looked askance at electricity and steam. Saddle and spur were his rocks of safety.

The man whom he had shot was a stranger to him. But the Kid knew that he was of the Coralitos outfit from Hidalgo; and that the punchers from that ranch were more relentless and vengeful than Kentucky feudists when wrong or harm was done to one of them. So, with the wisdom that has characterized many great fighters, the Kid decided to pile up as many leagues as possible of chaparral and pear between himself and the retaliation of the Coralitos bunch.

Near the station was a store; and near the store, scattered among the mesquite and elms, stood the saddled horses of the customers. Most of them waited, half asleep, with sagging limbs and drooping heads. But one, a long-legged roan with a curved neck, snorted and pawed the turf. Him the Kid mounted, gripped with his knees, and slapped gently with the owner's own quirt.

If the slaying of the temerarious card-player had cast a cloud over the Kid's standing as a good and true citizen, this last act of his veiled his figure in the darkest shadows of disrepute. On the Rio Grande border if you take a man's life you sometimes take trash; but if you take his horse, you take a thing the loss of which renders him poor, indeed; and which enriches you not — if you are caught. For the Kid there was no turning back now.

With the springing roan under him he felt little care or uneasiness. After a five-mile gallop he drew in to the plainsman's jogging trot, and rode northeastward toward the Nueces River bottoms. He knew the country well — its most tortuous and obscure trails through the great wilderness of brush and pear, and its camps and lonesome ranches where one might find safe entertainment. Always he bore to the east; for the Kid had never seen the ocean, and he had a fancy to lay his hand upon the mane of the great Gulf, the gamesome colt of the greater waters.

So after three days he stood on the shore at Corpus Christi, and looked out across the gentle ripples of a quiet sea.

Captain Boone, of the schooner *Flyaway*, stood near his skiff, which one of his crew was guarding in the surf. When ready to sail he had discovered that one of the necessaries of life, in the parallelogrammatic shape of plug tobacco, had been forgotten. A sailor had been dispatched for the missing cargo. Meanwhile the captain paced the sands, chewing profanely at his pocket store.

A slim, wiry youth in high-heeled boots came down to the water's edge. His face was boyish, but with a premature severity that hinted at a man's experience. His complexion was naturally dark; and the sun and wind of an outdoor life had burned it to a coffee-brown. His hair was as black and straight as an Indian's; his face had not yet been upturned to the humiliation of a razor; his eyes were a cold and steady blue. He carried his left arm somewhat away from his body, for pearl-handled .45s are frowned upon by town marshals, and are a little bulky when packed in the left armhole of one's vest. He looked beyond Captain Boone at the gulf with the impersonal and expressionless dignity of a Chinese emperor.

"Thinkin' of buyin' that 'ar gulf, buddy?" asked the captain, made sarcastic by his narrow escape from the tobaccoless voyage.

"Why, no," said the Kid gently, "I reckon not. I never saw it before. I was just looking at it. Not thinking of selling it, are you?"

"Not this trip," said the captain. "I'll send it to you C. O. D. when I get back to Buenas Tierras. Here comes that capstan-footed lubber with the chewin'. I ought to've weighed anchor an hour ago."

"Is that your ship out there?" asked the Kid.

"Why, yes," answered the captain, "if you want to call a schooner a ship, and I don't mind lyin'. But you better say Miller and Gonzales, owners, and ordinarily plain, Billy-de-damned old Samuel K. Boone, skipper."

"Where are you going to?" asked the refugee.

"Buenas Tierras, coast of South America — I forget what they called the country the last time I was there. Cargo — lumber, corrugated iron, and machetes."

"What kind of a country is it?" asked the Kid — "hot or cold?"

"Warmish, buddy," said the captain. "But a regular Paradise Lost for elegance of scenery and be-yooty of geography. Ye're wakened every morning by the sweet singin' of red birds with seven purple tails, and the sighin' of breezes in the posies and roses. And the inhabitants never work, for they can reach out and pick steamer baskets of the choicest hothouse fruit without gettin' out of bed. And there's no Sunday and no ice and no rent and no troubles and no use and no nothin'. It's a great country for a man to go to sleep with, and wait for somethin' to turn up. The bananys and oranges and hurricanes and pineapples that ye eat comes from there."

"That sounds to me!" said the Kid, at last betraying interest. "What'll the expressage be to take me out there with you?"

"Twenty-four dollars," said Captain Boone; "grub and transportation. Second cabin. I haven't got a first cabin."

"You've got my company," said the Kid, pulling out a buckskin bag.

With three hundred dollars he had gone to Laredo for his regular "blowout." The duel in Valdo's had cut short his season of hilarity, but it had left him with nearly $200 for aid in the flight that it had made necessary.

"All right, buddy," said the captain. "I hope your ma won't blame me for this little childish escapade of yours." He beckoned to one of the boat's crew. "Let Sanchez lift you out to the skiff so you won't get your feet wet."

Thacker, the United States consul at Buenas Tierras, was not yet drunk. It was only eleven o'clock; and he never arrived at his desired state of beatitude — a state where he sang ancient maudlin vaudeville songs and pelted his screaming parrot with banana peels — until the middle of the afternoon. So, when he looked up from his hammock at the sound of a slight cough, and saw the Kid standing in the door of the consulate, he was still in a condition to extend the hospitality and courtesy due from the representative of a great nation. "Don't disturb yourself," said the Kid easily. "I just dropped in. They told me it was customary to light at your camp before starting in to round up the town. I just came in on a ship from Texas."

"Glad to see you, Mr. —" said the consul.

The Kid laughed.

"Sprague Dalton," he said. "It sounds funny to me to hear it. I'm called the Llano Kid in the Rio Grande country."

"I'm Thacker," said the consul. "Take that cane-bottom chair. Now if you've come to invest, you want somebody to advise you. These natives will cheat you out of the gold in your teeth if you don't understand their ways. Try a cigar?"

"Much obliged," said the Kid, "but if it wasn't for my corn shucks and the little bag in my back pocket I couldn't live a minute." He took out his "makings," and rolled a cigarette.

"They speak Spanish here," said the consul. "You'll need an interpreter. If there's anything I can do, why, I'd be delighted. If you're buying fruit lands or looking for a concession of any sort, you'll want somebody who knows the ropes to look out for you."

"I speak Spanish," said the Kid, "about nine times better than I do English. Everybody speaks it on the range where I come from. And I'm not in the market for anything."

"You speak Spanish?" said Thacker, thoughtfully. He regarded the Kid absorbedly.

"You look like a Spaniard, too," he continued. "And you're from Texas. And you can't be more than twenty or twenty-one. I wonder if you've got any nerve."

"You got a deal of some kind to put through?" asked the Texan, with unexpected shrewdness.

"Are you open to a proposition?" said Thacker.

"What's the use to deny it?" said the Kid. "I got into a little gun frolic down in Laredo, and plugged a white man. There wasn't any Mexican handy. And I come down to your parrot-and-monkey range just for to smell the morning-glories and marigolds. Now, do you *sabe?*"

Thacker got up and closed the door.

"Let me see your hand," he said.

He took the Kid's left hand, and examined the back of it closely.

"I can do it," he said, excitedly. "Your flesh is as hard as wood and as healthy as a baby's. It will heal in a week."

"If it's a fist fight you want to back me for," said the Kid, "don't put your money up yet. Make it gun work, and I'll keep you company. But no bare-handed scrapping, like ladies at a tea-party, for me."

"It's easier than that," said Thacker. "Just step here, will you?"

Through the window he pointed to a two-story white-stuccoed house with wide galleries rising amid the deep-green tropical foliage on a wooded hill that sloped gently from the sea.

"In that house," said Thacker, "a fine old Castilian gentleman and his wife are yearning to gather you into their arms and fill your pockets with money. Old Santos Urique lives there. He owns half the gold-mines in the country."

"You haven't been eating loco weed, have you?" asked the Kid.

"Sit down again," said Thacker, "and I'll tell you. Twelve years ago they lost a kid. No, he didn't die — although most of 'em do from drinking the surface water. He was a wild little devil, even if he wasn't but eight years old. Everybody knows about it. Some Americans who were through here prospecting for gold had letters to Señor Urique, and the boy was a favorite with them. They filled his head with big stories about the States; and about a month after they left, the kid disappeared, too. He was supposed to have stowed himself away among the banana bunches on a fruit steamer, and gone to New Orleans. He was seen once afterwards in Texas, it was thought, but they never heard anything more of him. Old Urique has spent thousands of dollars having him looked for. The madam was broken up worst of all. The kid was her life. She wears mourning yet. But they say she believes he'll come back to her some day, and never gives up hope. On the back of the boy's left hand was tattooed a flying eagle carrying a spear in his claws. That's old Urique's coat of arms or something that he inherited in Spain."

The Kid raised his left hand slowly and gazed at it curiously.

"That's it," said Thacker, reaching behind the official desk for his bottle of smuggled brandy. "You're not so slow. I can do it. What was I consul at Sandakan for? I never knew till now. In a week I'll have the eagle bird with the frog-sticker blended in so you'd think you were born with it. I brought a set of the needles and ink just because I was sure you'd drop in some day, Mr. Dalton."

"Oh, hell," said the Kid. "I thought I told you my name!"

"All right, 'Kid,' then. It won't be that long. How does 'Señorito Urique' sound, for a change?"

"I never played son any that I remember of," said the Kid. "If I had any parents to mention they went over the divide about the time I gave my first bleat. What is the plan of your round-up?"

Thacker leaned back against the wall and held his glass up to the light.

"We've come now," said he, "to the question of how far you're willing to go in a little matter of the sort."

"I told you why I came down here," said the Kid simply.

"A good answer," said the consul. "But you won't have to go that far. Here's the scheme. After I get the trade-mark tattooed on your hand I'll notify old Urique. In the meantime I'll furnish you with all of the family history I can find out, so you can be studying up points to talk about. You've got the looks, you speak the Spanish, you know the facts, you can tell about Texas, you've got the tattoo mark. When I notify them that the rightful heir has returned and is waiting to know whether he will be received and pardoned, what will happen? They'll simply rush down here and fall on your neck, and the curtain goes down for refreshments and a stroll in the lobby."

"I'm waiting," said the Kid. "I haven't had my saddle off in your camp long, pardner, and I never met you before; but if you intend to let it go at a parental blessing, why, I'm mistaken in my man, that's all."

"Thanks," said the consul. "I haven't met anybody in a long time that keeps up with an argument as well as you do. The rest of it is simple. If they take you in only for a while it's long enough. Don't give 'em time to hunt up the strawberry mark on your left shoulder. Old Urique keeps anywhere from $50,000 to $100,000 in his house all the time in a little safe that you could open with a shoe buttoner. Get it. My skill as a tattooer is worth half the boodle. We go halves and catch a tramp steamer for Rio. Let the United States go to pieces if it can't get along without my services. *Qué dice, señor?*"

"It sounds to me!" said the Kid, nodding his head. "I'm out for the dust."

"All right, then," said Thacker. "You'll have to keep close until we get the bird on you. You can live in the back room here. I do my own cooking, and I'll make you as comfortable as a parsimonious government will allow me."

Thacker had set the time at a week, but it was two weeks before the design that he patiently tattooed upon the Kid's hand was to his notion. And then Thacker called a *muchacho*, and dispatched this note to the intended victim:

EL SENOR DON SANTOS URIQUE,
La Casa Blanca.
MY DEAR SIR:
I beg permission to inform you that there is in my house as a temporary guest a young man who arrived in Buenas Tierras from the United States some days ago. Without wishing to excite any hopes that may not be realized, I think there is a possibility of his being your long-absent son. It might be well for you to call and see him. If he is, it is my opinion that his intention was to return to his home, but upon arriving here, his courage failed him from doubts as to how he would be received. Your true servant,

THOMPSON THACKER.

Half an hour afterward — quick time for Buenas Tierras — Señor Urique's ancient landau drove to the consul's door, with the bare-footed coachman beating and shouting at the team of fat, awkward horses.

A tall man with a white moustache alighted, and assisted to the ground a lady who was dressed and veiled in unrelieved black.

The two hastened inside, and were met by Thacker with his best diplomatic bow. By his desk stood a slender young man with clear-cut, sunbrowned features and smoothly brushed black hair.

Señora Urique threw back her heavy veil with a quick gesture. She was past middle age, and her hair was beginning to silver, but her full, proud figure and clear olive skin retained traces of the beauty peculiar to the Basque province. But, once you had seen her eyes, and comprehended the great sadness that was revealed in their deep shadows and hopeless expression, you saw that the woman lived only in some memory.

She bent upon the young man a long look of the most agonized questioning. Then her great black eyes turned, and her gaze rested upon his left hand. And then with a sob, not loud, but seeming to shake the room, she cried *"Hijo mío!"* and caught the Llano Kid to her heart.

A month afterward the Kid came to the consulate in response to a message sent by Thacker.

He looked the young Spanish caballero. His clothes were imported, and the wiles of the jewellers had not been spent upon him in vain. A more than respectable diamond shone on his finger as he rolled a shuck cigarette.

"What's doing?" asked Thacker.

"Nothing much," said the Kid calmly. "I eat my first iguana steak to-day. They're them big lizards, you *sabe?* I reckon, though, that frijoles and side bacon would do me about as well. Do you care for iguanas, Thacker?"

"No, nor for some other kinds of reptiles," said Thacker.

It was three in the afternoon, and in another hour he would be in his state of beatitude.

"It's time you were making good, sonny," he went on, with an ugly look on his reddened face. "You're not playing up to me square. You've been the prodigal son for four weeks now, and you could have had veal for every meal on a gold dish if you'd wanted it. Now, Mr. Kid, do you think it's right to leave me out so long on a husk diet? What's the trouble? Don't you get your filial eyes on anything that looks like cash in the Casa Blanca? Don't tell me you don't. Everybody knows where old Urique keeps his stuff. It's U. S. currency, too; he don't accept anything else. What's doing? Don't say 'nothing' this time."

"Why, sure," said the Kid, admiring his diamond, "there's plenty of money up there. I'm no judge of collateral in bunches, but I will undertake for to say that I've seen the rise of $50,000 at a time in that tin grub box that my adopted father calls his safe. And he lets me carry the key sometimes just to show me that he knows I'm the real little Francisco that strayed from the herd a long time ago."

"Well, what are you waiting for?" asked Thacker angrily. "Don't you forget that I can upset your apple-cart any day I want to. If old

Urique knew you were an impostor, what sort of things would happen to you? Oh, you don't know this country, Mr. Texas Kid. The laws here have got mustard spread between 'em. These people here'd stretch you out like a frog that had been stepped on, and give you about fifty sticks at every corner of the plaza. And they'd wear every stick out, too. What was left of you they'd feed to alligators."

"I might as well tell you now, pardner," said the Kid, sliding down low on his steamer chair, "that things are going to stay just as they are. They're about right now."

"What do you mean?" asked Thacker, rattling the bottom of his glass on his desk.

"The scheme's off," said the Kid. "And whenever you have the pleasure of speaking to me address me as Don Francisco Urique. I'll guarantee I'll answer to it. We'll let Colonel Urique keep his money. His little tin safe is as good as the time-locker in the First National Bank of Laredo as far as you and me are concerned."

"You're going to throw me down, then, are you?" said the consul.

"Sure," said the Kid, cheerfully. "Throw you down. That's it. And now I'll tell you why. The first night I was up at the colonel's house they introduced me to a bedroom. No blankets on the floor — a real room, with a bed and things in it. And before I was asleep, in comes this artificial mother of mine and tucks in the covers. 'Panchito,' she says, 'my little lost one, God has brought you back to me. I bless His name forever.' It was that, or some truck like that, she said. And down comes a drop or two of rain and hits me on the nose. And all that stuck by me, Mr. Thacker. And it's been that way ever since. And it's got to stay that way. Don't you think that it's for what's in it for me, either, that I say so. If you have any such ideas keep 'em to yourself. I haven't had much truck with women in my life, and no mothers to speak of, but here's a lady that we've got to keep fooled. Once she stood it; twice she won't. I'm a low-down wolf, and the devil may have sent me on this trail instead of God, but I'll travel it to the end. And now, don't forget that I'm Don Francisco Urique whenever you happen to mention my name."

"I'll expose you to-day, you — you double-dyed traitor," stammered Thacker.

The Kid arose and, without violence, took Thacker by the throat with a hand of steel, and shoved him slowly into a corner. Then he drew from under his left arm his pearl-handled .45 and poked the cold muzzle of it against the consul's mouth.

"I told you why I come here," he said, with his old freezing smile. "If I leave here, you'll be the reason. Never forget it, pardner. Now, what is my name?"

"Er — Don Francisco Urique," gasped Thacker.

From outside came a sound of wheels, and the shouting of someone, and the sharp whacks of a wooden whipstock upon the backs of fat horses.

The Kid put up his gun, and walked toward the door. But he turned again and came back to the trembling Thacker, and held up his left hand with its back toward the consul.

"There's one more reason," he said, slowly, "why things have got to stand as they are. The fellow I killed in Laredo had one of them same pictures on his left hand."

Outside, the ancient landau of Don Santos Urique rattled to the door. The coachman ceased his bellowing. Señora Urique, in a voluminous gay gown of white lace and flying ribbons, leaned forward with a happy look in her great soft eyes.

"Are you within, dear son?" she called, in rippling Castilian.

"*Madre mia, yo vengo* [Mother, I come]," answered the young Don Francisco Urique.

ONE DOLLAR'S WORTH

THE judge of the United States court of the district lying along Rio Grande border found the following letter one morning in his mail:

JUDGE:
   When you sent me up for four years you made a talk. Among other hard things, you called me a rattlesnake. Maybe I am one — anyhow, you hear me rattling now. One year after I got to the pen, my daughter died of — well, they said it was poverty and the disgrace together. You've got a daughter, Judge, and I'm going to make you know how it feels to lose one. And I'm going to bite that district attorney that spoke against me. I'm free now, and I guess I've turned to rattlesnake all right. I feel like one. I don't say much, but this is my rattle. Look out what I strike.

Yours respectfully,
RATTLESNAKE

Judge Derwent threw the letter carelessly aside. It was nothing new to receive such epistles from desperate men whom he had been called upon to judge. He felt no alarm. Later on he showed the letter to Littlefield, the young district attorney, for Littlefield's name was included in the threat, and the judge was punctilious in matters between himself and his fellow men.

Littlefield honored the rattle of the writer, as far as it concerned himself, with a smile of contempt; but he frowned a little over the reference to the Judge's daughter, for he and Nancy Derwent were to be married in the fall.

Littlefield went to the clerk of the court and looked over the records with him. They decided that the letter might have been sent by Mexico Sam, a half-breed border desperado who had been imprisoned for manslaughter four years before. Then official duties crowded the matter from his mind, and the rattle of the revengeful serpent was forgotten.

Court was in session at Brownsville. Most of the cases to be tried were charges of smuggling, counterfeiting, post-office robberies, and violations of Federal laws along the border. One case was that of a young Mexican, Rafael Ortiz, who had been rounded up by a clever deputy marshal in the act of passing a counterfeit silver dollar. He had

been suspected of many such deviations from rectitude, but this was
the first time that anything provable had been fixed upon him. Ortiz
languished cozily in jail, smoking brown cigarettes and waiting for
trial. Kilpatrick, the deputy, brought the counterfeit dollar and
handed it to the district attorney in his office in the court-house. The
deputy and a reputable druggist were prepared to swear that Ortiz
paid for a bottle of medicine with it. The coin was a poor counterfeit,
soft, dull-looking, and made principally of lead. It was the day before
the morning on which the docket would reach the case of Ortiz, and
the district attorney was preparing himself for the trial.

"Not much need of having in high-priced experts to prove the
coin's queer, is there, Kil?" smiled Littlefield, as he thumped the dollar down upon the table, where it fell with no more ring than would
have come from a lump of putty.

"I guess the Mexican's as good as behind the bars," said the deputy,
easing up his holsters. "You've got him dead. If it had been just one
time, these Mexicans can't tell good money from bad; but this little
yaller rascal belongs to a gang of counterfeiters, I know. This is the
first time I've been able to catch him doing the trick. He's got a girl
down there in them Mexican *jacales* on the river bank. I seen her one
day when I was watching him. She's as pretty as a red heifer in a flower
bed."

Littlefield shoved the counterfeit dollar into his pocket, and slipped
his memoranda of the case into an envelope. Just then a bright, winsome face, as frank and jolly as a boy's, appeared in the doorway, and
in walked Nancy Derwent.

"Oh, Bob, didn't court adjourn at twelve to-day until to-morrow?"
she asked of Littlefield.

"It did," said the district attorney, "and I'm very glad of it. I've got
a lot of rulings to look up, and —"

"Now, that's just like you. I wonder you and Father don't turn to
law books or rulings or something! I want you to take me out plover-
shooting this afternoon. Long Prairie is just alive with them. Don't say
no, please! I want to try my new twelve-bore hammerless. I've sent to
the livery stable to engage Fly and Bess for the buckboard; they stand
fire so nicely. I was sure you would go."

They were to be married in the fall. The glamour was at its height.
The plovers won the day — or, rather, the afternoon — over the calf-
bound authorities. Littlefield began to put his papers away.

There was a knock at the door. Kilpatrick answered it. A beautiful,
dark-eyed girl with a skin tinged with the faintest lemon color walked

into the room. A black shawl was thrown over her head and wound once around her neck.

She began to talk in Spanish, a voluble, mournful stream of melancholy music. Littlefield did not understand Spanish. The deputy did, and he translated her talk by portions, at intervals holding up his hands to check the flow of her words.

"She came to see you, Mr. Littlefield. Her name's Joya Treviñas. She wants to see you about — well, she's mixed up with that Rafael Ortiz. She's his — she's his girl. She says he's innocent. She says she made the money and got him to pass it. Don't you believe her, Mr. Littlefield. That's the way with these Mexican girls; they'll lie, steal, or kill for a fellow when they get stuck on him. Never trust a woman that's in love!"

"Mr. Kilpatrick!"

Nancy Derwent's indignant exclamation caused the deputy to flounder for a moment in attempting to explain that he had misquoted his own sentiments, and then he went on with the translation:

"She says she's willing to take his place in the jail if you'll let him out. She says she was down sick with the fever, and the doctor said she'd die if she didn't have medicine. That's why he passed the lead dollar on the drug store. She says it saved her life. This Rafael seems to be her honey, all right; there's a lot of stuff in her talk about love and such things that you don't want to hear."

It was an old story to the district attorney.

"Tell her," said he, "that I can do nothing. The case comes up in the morning, and he will have to make his fight before the court."

Nancy Derwent was not so hardened. She was looking with sympathetic interest at Joya Treviñas and at Littlefield alternately. The deputy repeated the district attorney's words to the girl. She spoke a sentence or two in a low voice, pulled her shawl closely about her face, and left the room.

"What did she say then?" asked the district attorney.

"Nothing special," said the deputy. "She said: 'If the life of the one' — let's see how it went — '*Si la vida de ella a quien tu amas* — if the life of the girl you love is ever in danger, remember Rafael Ortiz.' "

Kilpatrick strolled out through the corridor in the direction of the marshal's office.

"Can't you do anything for them, Bob?" asked Nancy. "It's such a little thing — just one counterfeit dollar — to ruin the happiness of two lives! She was in danger of death, and he did it to save her. Doesn't the law know the feeling of pity?"

"It hasn't a place in jurisprudence, Nan," said Littlefield, "especially *in re* the district attorney's duty. I'll promise you that prosecution will not be vindictive; but the man is as good as convicted when the case is called. Witnesses will swear to his passing the bad dollar which I have in my pocket at this moment as 'Exhibit A.' There are no Mexicans on the jury, and it will vote the prisoner guilty without leaving the box."

The plover-shooting was fine that afternoon, and in the excitement of the sport the case of Rafael and the grief of Joya Treviñas was forgotten. The district attorney and Nancy Derwent drove out from the town three miles along a smooth, grassy road, and then struck across a rolling prairie toward a heavy line of timber on Piedra Creek. Beyond this creek lay Long Prairie, the favorite haunt of the plover. As they were nearing the creek they heard the galloping of a horse to their right, and saw a man with black hair and a swarthy face riding toward the woods at a tangent, as if he had come up behind them.

"I've seen that fellow somewhere," said Littlefield, who had a memory for faces, "but I can't exactly place him. Some ranchman, I suppose, taking a short cut home."

They spent an hour on Long Prairie, shooting from the buckboard. Nancy Derwent, an active, outdoor Western girl, was pleased with her twelve-bore. She had bagged within two brace of her companion's score.

They started homeward at a gentle trot. When within a hundred yards of Piedra Creek a man rode out of the timber directly toward them.

"It looks like the man we saw coming over," remarked Miss Derwent.

As the distance between them lessened, the district attorney suddenly pulled up his team sharply, with his eyes fixed upon the advancing horseman. That individual had drawn a Winchester from its scabbard on his saddle and thrown it over his arm.

"Now I know you, Mexico Sam!" muttered Littlefield to himself. "It *was* you who shook your rattles in that gentle epistle."

Mexico Sam did not leave things long in doubt. He had a nice eye in all matters relating to firearms, so when he was within good rifle range, but outside of danger from No. 8 shot, he threw up his Winchester and opened fire upon the occupants of the buckboard.

The first shot cracked the back of the seat within the two-inch space between the shoulders of Littlefield and Miss Derwent. The next went through the dashboard and Littlefield's trouser leg.

The district attorney hustled Nancy out of the buckboard to the ground. She was a little pale, but asked no questions. She had the frontier instinct that accepts conditions in an emergency without superfluous argument. They kept their guns in hand, and Littlefield hastily gathered some handfuls of cartridges from the pasteboard box on the seat and crowded them into his pockets.

"Keep behind the horses, Nan," he commanded. "That fellow is a ruffian I sent to prison once. He's trying to get even. He knows our shot won't hurt him at that distance."

"All right, Bob," said Nancy, steadily. "I'm not afraid. But you come close, too — whoa, Bess; stand still, now!"

She stroked Bess's mane. Littlefield stood with his gun ready, praying that the desperado would come within range.

But Mexico Sam was playing his vendetta along safe lines. He was a bird of different feather from the plover. His accurate eye drew an imaginary line of circumference around the area of danger from birdshot, and upon this line he rode. His horse wheeled to the right, and as his victims rounded to the safe side of their equine breastwork he sent a ball through the district attorney's hat. Once he miscalculated in making a detour, and overstepped his margin. Littlefield's gun flashed, and Mexico Sam ducked his head to the harmless patter of the shot. A few of them stung his horse, which pranced promptly back to the safety line.

The desperado fired again. A little cry came from Nancy Derwent. Littlefield whirled, with blazing eyes, and saw the blood trickling down her cheek.

"I'm not hurt, Bob — only a splinter struck me. I think he hit one of the wheel-spokes."

"Lord!" groaned Littlefield. "If I only had a charge of buckshot!"

The ruffian got his horse still, and took careful aim. Fly gave a snort and fell in the harness, struck in the neck. Bess, now disabused of the idea that plover were being fired at, broke her traces and galloped wildly away. Mexican Sam sent a ball neatly through the fullness of Nancy Derwent's shooting jacket.

"Lie down — lie down!" snapped Littlefield. "Close to the horse — flat on the ground — so." He almost threw her upon the grass against the back of the recumbent Fly. Oddly enough, at that moment the words of the Mexican girl returned to his mind:

"If the life of the girl you love is ever in danger, remember Rafael Ortiz."

Littlefield uttered an exclamation.

"Open fire on him, Nan, across the horse's back! Fire as fast as you can! You can't hurt him, but keep him dodging shot for one minute while I try to work a little scheme."

Nancy gave a quick glance at Littlefield, and saw him take out his pocketknife and open it. Then she turned her face to obey orders, keeping up a rapid fire at the enemy.

Mexico Sam waited patiently until this innocuous fusillade ceased. He had plenty of time, and he did not care to risk the chance of a bird-shot in his eye if it could be avoided by a little caution. He pulled his heavy Stetson low down over his face until the shots ceased. Then he drew a little nearer, and fired with careful aim at what he could see of his victims above the fallen horse.

Neither of them moved. He urged his horse a few steps nearer. He saw the district attorney rise to one knee, and deliberately level his shotgun. He pulled his hat down and awaited the harmless rattle of the tiny pellets.

The shotgun blazed with a heavy report. Mexico Sam sighed, turned limp all over, and slowly fell from his horse — a dead rattlesnake.

At ten o'clock the next morning court opened, and the case of the United States *versus* Rafael Ortiz was called. The district attorney, with his arm in a sling, rose and addressed the court.

"May it please your honor," he said, "I desire to enter a *nolle pros.* in this case. Even though the defendant should be guilty, there is not sufficient evidence in the hands of the government to secure a conviction. The piece of counterfeit coin upon the identity of which the case was built is not now available as evidence. I ask, therefore, that the case be stricken off."

At the noon recess, Kilpatrick strolled into the district attorney's office.

"I've just been down to take a squint at old Mexico Sam," said the deputy. "They've got him laid out. Old Mexico was a tough outfit, I reckon. The boys was wonderin' down there what you shot him with. Some said it must have been nails. I never see a gun carrying anything to make holes like he had."

"I shot him," said the district attorney, "with Exhibit A of your counterfeiting case. Lucky thing for me — and somebody else — that it was as bad money as it was! It sliced up into slugs very nicely. Say, Kil, can't you go down to the *jacales* and find where that Mexican girl lives? Miss Derwent wants to know."

THE CABALLERO'S WAY

THE Cisco Kid had killed six men in more or less fair scrimmages, had murdered twice as many (mostly Mexicans), and had winged a large number whom he modestly forbore to count. Therefore a woman loved him.

The Kid was twenty-five, looked twenty; and a careful insurance company would have estimated the probable time of his demise at, say, twenty-six. His habitat was anywhere between the Frio and the Rio Grande. He killed for the love of it — because he was quick-tempered — to avoid arrest — for his own amusement — any reason that came to his mind would suffice. He had escaped capture because he could shoot five-sixths of a second sooner than any sheriff or ranger in the service, and because he rode a speckled roan horse that knew every cowpath in the mesquite and pear thickets from San Antonio to Matamoras.

Tonia Perez, the girl who loved the Cisco Kid, was half Carmen, half Madonna, and the rest — oh, yes, a woman who is half Carmen and half Madonna can always be something more — the rest, let us say, was humming-bird. She lived in a grass-roofed *jacal* near a little Mexican settlement at the Lone Wolf Crossing of the Frio. With her lived a father or grandfather, a lineal Aztec, somewhat less than a thousand years old, who herded a hundred goats and lived in a continuous drunken dream from drinking *mescal*. Back of the *jacal* a tremendous forest of bristling pear, twenty feet high at its worst, crowded almost to its door. It was along the bewildering maze of this spinous thicket that the speckled roan would bring the Kid to see his girl. And once, clinging like a lizard to the ridge-pole, high up under the peaked grass roof, he had heard Tonia, with her Madonna face and Carmen beauty and humming-bird soul, parley with the sheriff's posse, denying knowledge of her man in her soft *mélange* of Spanish and English.

One day the adjutant-general of the State, who is, *ex officio*, commander of the ranger forces, wrote some sarcastic lines to Captain Duval of Company X, stationed at Laredo, relative to the serene and undisturbed existence led by murderers and desperadoes in the said captain's territory.

The captain turned the color of brick dust under his tan, and forwarded the letter, after adding a few comments, per ranger Private Bill Adamson, to ranger Lieutenant Sandridge, camped at a water hole on the Nueces with a squad of five men in preservation of law and order.

Lieutenant Sandridge turned a beautiful *couleur de rose* through his ordinary strawberry complexion, tucked the letter in his hip pocket, and chewed off the end of his gamboge moustache.

The next morning he saddled his horse and rode alone to the Mexican settlement at the Lone Wolf Crossing of the Frio, twenty miles away.

Six feet two, blond as a Viking, quiet as a deacon, dangerous as a machine gun, Sandridge moved among the *jacales,* patiently seeking news of the Cisco Kid.

Far more than the law, the Mexicans dreaded the cold and certain vengeance of the lone rider that the ranger sought. It had been one of the Kid's pastimes to shoot Mexicans "to see them kick": if he demanded of them moribund Terpsichorean feats, simply that he might be entertained, what terrible and extreme penalties would be certain to follow should they anger him! One and all they lounged with upturned palms and shrugging shoulders, filling the air with *"quién sabes"* and denials of the Kid's acquaintance.

But there was a man named Fink who kept a store at the Crossing — a man of many nationalities, tongues, interests, and ways of thinking.

"No use to ask them Mexicans," he said to Sandridge. "They're afraid to tell. This *hombre* they call the Kid — Goodall is his name, ain't it? — he's been in my store once or twice. I have an idea you might run across him at — but I guess I don't keer to say, myself. I'm two seconds later in pulling a gun than I used to be and the difference is worth thinking about. But this Kid's got a half-Mexican girl at the Crossing that he comes to see. She lives in that *jacal* a hundred yards down the arroyo at the edge of the pear. Maybe she — no, I don't suppose she would, but that *jacal* would be a good place to watch, anyway."

Sandridge rode down to the *jacal* of Perez. The sun was low, and the broad shade of the great pear thicket already covered the grass-thatched hut. The goats were enclosed for the night in a brush corral near by. A few kids walked the top of it, nibbling the chaparral leaves. The old Mexican lay upon a blanket on the grass, already in a stupor from his mescal, and dreaming, perhaps, of the nights when he and Pizarro touched glasses to their New World fortunes — so old his wrinkled face seemed to proclaim him to be. And in the door of the *jacal* stood Tonia. And Lieutenant Sandridge sat in his saddle staring at her like a gannet agape at a sailorman.

The Cisco Kid was a vain person, as all eminent and successful assassins are, and his bosom would have been ruffled had he known that at a simple exchange of glances two persons, in whose minds he had been looming large, suddenly abandoned (at least for the time) all thought of him.

Never before had Tonia seen such a man as this. He seemed to be made of sunshine and blood-red tissue and clear weather. He seemed to illuminate the shadow of the pear when he smiled, as though the sun were rising again. The men she had known had been small and dark. Even the Kid, in spite of his achievements, was a stripling no larger than herself, with black straight hair and a cold marble face that chilled the noonday.

As for Tonia, though she sends description to the poorhouse, let her make a millionaire of your fancy. Her blue-black hair, smoothly divided in the middle and bound close to her head, and her large eyes full of the Latin melancholy, gave her the Madonna touch. Her motions and air spoke of the concealed fire and the desire to charm that she had inherited from the *gitanas* of the Basque province. As for the humming-bird part of her, that dwelt in her heart; you could not perceive it unless her bright red skirt and dark blue blouse gave you a symbolic hint of the vagarious bird.

The newly lighted sun-god asked for a drink of water. Tonia brought it from the red jar hanging under the brush shelter. Sandridge considered it necessary to dismount so as to lessen the trouble of her ministrations.

I play no spy; nor do I assume to master the thoughts of any human heart; but I assert, by the chronicler's right, that before a quarter of an hour had sped, Sandridge was teaching her how to plait a six-strand rawhide stake-rope, and Tonia had explained to him that were it not for her little English book that the peripatetic *padre* had given her and the little crippled *chivo*, that she fed from a bottle, she would be very, very lonely indeed.

Which leads to a suspicion that the Kid's fences needed repairing, and that the adjutant-general's sarcasm had fallen upon unproductive soil.

In his camp by the water hole Lieutenant Sandridge announced and reiterated his intention of either causing the Cisco Kid to nibble the black loam of the Frio country prairies or of haling him before a judge and jury. That sounded business-like. Twice a week he rode over to the Lone Wolf Crossing of the Frio, and directed Tonia's slim, slightly lemon-tinted fingers among the intricacies of the slowly growing lari-ata. A six-strand plait is hard to learn and easy to teach.

The ranger knew that he might find the Kid there at any visit. He kept his armament ready, and had a frequent eye for the pear thicket at the rear of the *jacal*. Thus he might bring down the kite and the humming-bird with one stone.

While the sunny-haired ornithologist was pursuing his studies the Cisco Kid was also attending to his professional duties. He moodily shot up a saloon in a small cow village on Quintana Creek, killed the town marshal (plugging him neatly in the centre of his tin badge), and then rode away, morose and unsatisfied. No true artist is uplifted by shooting an aged man carrying an old-style .38 bulldog.

On his way the Kid suddenly experienced the yearning that all men feel when wrong-doing loses its keen edge of delight. He yearned for the woman he loved to reassure him that she was his in spite of it. He wanted her to call his bloodthirstiness bravery and his cruelty devotion. He wanted Tonia to bring him water from the red jug under the brush shelter, and tell him how the *chivo* was thriving on the bottle.

The Kid turned the speckled roan's head up the ten-mile pear flat that stretches along the Arroyo Hondo until it ends at the Lone Wolf Crossing of the Frio. The roan whickered; for he had a sense of locality and direction equal to that of a belt-line street-car horse; and he knew he would soon be nibbling the rich mesquite grass at the end of a forty-foot stake rope while Ulysses rested his head in Circe's straw-roofed hut.

More weird and lonesome than the journey of an Amazonian explorer is the ride of one through a Texas pear flat. With dismal monotony and startling variety the uncanny and multiform shapes of the cacti lift their twisted trunks and fat, bristly hands to encumber the way. The demon plant, appearing to live without soil or rain, seems to taunt the parched traveler with its lush gray greenness. It warps itself a thousand times about what look to be open and inviting paths, only to lure the rider into blind and impassable spine-defended "bottoms of the bag," leaving him to retreat, if he can, with the points of the compass whirling in his head.

To be lost in the pear is to die almost the death of the thief on the cross, pierced by nails and with grotesque shapes of all the fiends hovering about.

But it was not so with the Kid and his mount. Winding, twisting, circling, tracing the most fantastic and bewildering trail ever picked out, the good roan lessened the distance to the Lone Wolf Crossing with every coil and turn that he made.

While they fared the Kid sang. He knew but one tune and he sang it, as he knew but one code and lived it, and but one girl and loved her. He was a single-minded man of conventional ideas. He had a voice like a coyote with bronchitis, but whenever he chose to sing his song he sang it. It was a conventional song of the camps and trail, running at its beginning as near as may be to these words:

> Don't you monkey with my Lulu girl
> Or I'll tell you what I'll do ——

and so on. The roan was inured to it, and did not mind.

But even the poorest singer will, after a certain time, gain his own consent to refrain from contributing to the world's noises. So the Kid, by the time he was within a mile or two of Tonia's *jacal*, had reluctantly allowed his song to die away — not because his vocal performance had become less charming to his own ears, but because his laryngeal muscles were aweary.

As though he were in a circus ring the speckled roan wheeled and danced through the labyrinth of pear until at length his rider knew by certain landmarks that the Lone Wolf Crossing was close at hand. Then, where the pear was thinner, he caught sight of the grass roof of the *jacal* and the hackberry tree on the edge of the arroyo. A few yards farther the Kid stopped the roan and gazed intently through the prickly openings. Then he dismounted, dropped the roan's reins, and proceeded on foot, stooping and silent, like an Indian. The roan, knowing his part, stood still, making no sound.

The Kid crept noiselessly to the very edge of the pear thicket and reconnoitered between the leaves of a clump of cactus.

Ten yards from his hiding-place, in the shade of the *jacal*, sat his Tonia calmly plaiting a raw-hide lariat. So far she might surely escape condemnation; women have been known, from time to time, to engage in more mischievous occupations. But if all must be told, there is to be added that her head reposed against the broad and comfortable chest of a tall red-and-yellow man, and that his arm was about her, guiding her nimble small fingers that required so many lessons at the intricate six-strand plait.

Sandridge glanced quickly at the dark mass of pear when he heard a slight squeaking sound that was not altogether unfamiliar. A gun-scabbard will make that sound when one grasps the handle of a six-shooter suddenly. But the sound was not repeated; and Tonia's fingers needed close attention.

And then, in the shadow of death, they began to talk of their love; and in the still July afternoon every word they uttered reached the ears of the Kid.

"Remember, then," said Tonia, "you must not come again until I send for you. Soon he will be here. A *vaquero* at the *tienda* said to-day he saw him on the Guadalupe three days ago. When he is that near he always comes. If he comes and finds you here he will kill you. So, for my sake, you must come no more until I send you the word."

"All right," said the ranger. "And then what?"

"And then," said the girl, "you must bring your men here and kill him. If not, he will kill you."

"He ain't a man to surrender, that's sure," said Sandridge. "It's kill or be killed for the officer that goes up against Mr. Cisco Kid."

"He must die," said the girl. "Otherwise there will not be any peace in the world for thee and me. He has killed many. Let him so die. Bring your men, and give him no chance to escape."

"You used to think right much of him," said Sandridge.

Tonia dropped the lariat, twisted herself around, and curved a lemon-tinted arm over the ranger's shoulder.

"But then," she murmured in liquid Spanish, "I had not beheld thee, thou great, red mountain of a man! And thou art kind and good, as well as strong. Could one choose him, knowing thee? Let him die; for then I will not be filled with fear by day and night lest he hurt thee or me."

"How can I know when he comes?" asked Sandridge.

"When he comes," said Tonia, "he remains two days, sometimes three. Gregorio, the small son of old Luisa, the *lavandera,* has a swift pony. I will write a letter to thee and send it by him, saying how it will be best to come upon him. By Gregorio will the letter come. And bring many men with thee, and have much care, oh, dear red one, for the rattlesnake is not quicker to strike than is 'El Chivato,' as they call him, to send a ball from his *pistola.*"

"The Kid's handy with his gun, sure enough," admitted Sandridge, "but when I come for him I shall come alone. I'll get him by myself or not at all. The Cap wrote one or two things to me that make me want to do the trick without any help. You let me know when Mr. Kid arrives, and I'll do the rest."

"I will send you the message by the boy Gregorio," said the girl. "I knew you were braver than that small slayer of men who never smiles. How could I ever have thought I cared for him?"

It was time for the ranger to ride back to his camp on the water hole.

Before he mounted his horse he raised the slight form of Tonia with one arm high from the earth for a parting salute. The drowsy stillness of the torpid summer air still lay thick upon the dreaming afternoon. The smoke from the fire in the *jacal,* where the *frijoles* blubbered in the iron pot, rose straight as a plumb-line above the clay-daubed chimney. No sound or movement disturbed the serenity of the dense pear thicket ten yards away.

When the form of Sandridge disappeared, loping his big dun down the steep banks of the Frio crossing, the Kid crept back to his own horse, mounted him, and rode back along the tortuous trail he had come.

But not far. He stopped and waited in the silent depths of the pear until half an hour had passed. And then Tonia heard the high, untrue notes of his unmusical singing coming nearer and nearer; and she ran to the edge of the pear to meet him.

The Kid seldom smiled; but he smiled and waved his hat when he saw her. He dismounted, and his girl sprang into his arms. The Kid looked at her fondly. His thick hair clung to his head like a wrinkled mat. The meeting brought a slight ripple of some undercurrent of feeling to his smooth, dark face that was usually as motionless as a clay mask.

"How's my girl?" he asked, holding her close.

"Sick of waiting so long for you, dear one," she answered. "My eyes are dim with always gazing into that devil's pincushion through which you come. And I can see into it such a little way, too. But you are here, beloved one, and I will not scold. *Qué mal muchacho!* not to come to see your *alma* more often. Go in and rest, and let me water your horse and stake him with the long rope. There is cool water in the jar for you."

The Kid kissed her affectionately.

"Not if the court knows itself do I let a lady stake my horse for me," said he. "But if you'll run in, *chica*, and throw a pot of coffee together while I attend to the *caballo*, I'll be a good deal obliged."

Besides his marksmanship the Kid had another attribute for which he admired himself greatly. He was *muy cabellero*, as the Mexicans express it, where the ladies were concerned. For them he had always gentle words and consideration. He could not have spoken a harsh word to a woman. He might ruthlessly slay their husbands and brothers, but he could not have laid the weight of a finger in anger upon a woman. Wherefore many of that interesting division of humanity who had come under the spell of his politeness declared their disbelief in the stories circulated about Mr. Kid. One shouldn't believe everything one heard, they said. When confronted by their indignant men folk with proof of the *caballero's* deeds of infamy, they said maybe he had been driven to it, and that he knew how to treat a lady, anyhow.

Considering this extremely courteous idiosyncrasy of the Kid and the pride that he took in it, one can perceive that the solution of the problem that was presented to him by what he saw and heard from his hiding-place in the pear that afternoon (at least as to one of the actors) must have been obscured by difficulties. And yet one could not think of the Kid overlooking little matters of that kind.

At the end of the short twilight they gathered around a supper of *frijoles*, goat steaks, canned peaches, and coffee, by the light of a lantern in the *jacal*. Afterward, the ancestor, his flock corralled, smoked a cigarette and became a mummy in a gray blanket. Tonia washed the few dishes while the Kid dried them with the flour-sacking towel. Her eyes shone; she chatted volubly of the inconsequent happenings of her small world since the Kid's last visit; it was as all his other homecomings had been.

Then outside Tonia swung in a grass hammock with her guitar and sang sad *canciones de amor*.

"Do you love me just the same, old girl?" asked the Kid, hunting for his cigarette papers.

"Always the same, little one," said Tonia, her dark eyes lingering upon him.

"I must go over to Fink's," said the Kid, rising, "for some tobacco. I thought I had another sack in my coat. I'll be back in a quarter of an hour."

"Hasten," said Tonia, "and tell me — how long shall I call you my own this time? Will you be gone again to-morrow, leaving me to grieve, or will you be longer with your Tonia?"

"Oh, I might stay two or three days this trip," said the Kid, yawning. "I've been on the dodge for a month, and I'd like to rest up."

He was gone half an hour for his tobacco. When he returned Tonia was still lying in the hammock.

"It's funny," said the Kid, "how I feel. I feel like there was somebody lying behind every bush and tree waiting to shoot me. I never had mullygrubs like them before. Maybe it's one of them presumptions. I've got half a notion to light out in the morning before day. The Guadalupe country is burning up about that old Dutchman I plugged down there."

"You are not afraid — no one could make my brave little one fear."

"Well, I haven't been usually regarded as a jack-rabbit when it comes to scrapping; but I don't want a posse smoking me out when I'm in your *jacal*. Somebody might get hurt that oughtn't to."

"Remain with your Tonia — no one will find you here."

The Kid looked keenly into the shadows up and down the arroyo and toward the dim lights of the Mexican village.

"I'll see how it looks later on," was his decision.

At midnight a horseman rode into the rangers' camp, blazing his way by noisy "halloes" to indicate a pacific mission. Sandridge and one or two others turned out to investigate the row. The rider announced himself to be Domingo Sales, from the Lone Wolf Crossing. He bore a letter for Señor Sandridge. Old Luisa, the *lavandera*, had persuaded him to bring it, he said, her son Gregorio being too ill of a fever to ride.

Sandridge lighted the camp lantern and read the letter. These were its words:

DEAR ONE: He has come. Hardly had you ridden away when he came out of the pear. When he first talked he said he would stay three days or more. Then as it grew later he was like a wolf or a fox, and walked about without rest, looking and listening. Soon he said he must leave before daylight when it is dark and stillest. And then he seemed to suspect that I be not true to him. He looked at me so strange that I am frightened. I swear to him that I love him, his own Tonia. Last of all he said I must prove to him I am true. He thinks that even now men are waiting to kill him as he rides from my house. To escape he says he will dress in my clothes, my red skirt and the blue waist I wear and the brown mantilla over the head, and thus ride away. But before that he says that I must put on his clothes, his *pantalones* and *camisa* and hat, and ride away on his horse from the *jacal* as far as the big road beyond the crossing and back again. This before he goes, so he can tell if I am true and if men are hidden to shoot him. It is a terrible thing. An hour before daybreak this is to be. Come, my dear one, and kill this man and take me for your Tonia. Do not try to take hold of him alive, but kill him quickly. Knowing all, you should do that. You must come long before the time and hide yourself in the little shed near the *jacal* where the wagon and saddles are kept. It is dark in there. He will wear my red skirt and blue waist and brown mantilla. I send you a hundred kisses. Come surely and shoot quickly and straight.

THINE OWN TONIA.

Sandridge quickly explained to his men the official part of the missive. The rangers protested against his going alone.

"I'll get him easy enough," said the lieutenant. "The girl's got him trapped. And don't even think he'll get the drop on me."

Sandridge saddled his horse and rode to the Lone Wolf Crossing. He tied his big dun in a clump of brush on the arroyo, took his Winchester from its scabbard, and carefully approached the Perez *jacal*. There was only the half of a high moon drifted over by ragged, milk-white gulf clouds.

The wagon-shed was an excellent place for ambush; and the ranger got inside it safely. In the black shadow of the brush shelter in front of the *jacal* he could see a horse tied and hear him impatiently pawing the hard-trodden earth.

He waited almost an hour before two figures came out of the *jacal*. One, in man's clothes, quickly mounted the horse and galloped past the wagon-shed toward the crossing and village. And then the other figure, in skirt, waist, and mantilla over its head, stepped out into the faint moonlight, gazing after the rider. Sandridge thought he would take his chance then before Tonia rode back. He fancied she might not care to see it.

"Throw up your hands," he ordered, loudly, stepping out of the wagon-shed with his Winchester at his shoulder.

There was a quick turn of the figure, but no movement to obey, so the ranger pumped in the bullets — one — two — three — and then twice more; for you never could be too sure of bringing down the Cisco Kid. There was no danger of missing at ten paces, even in the half moonlight.

The old ancestor, asleep on his blanket, was awakened by the shots. Listening further, he heard a great cry from some man in mortal distress or anguish, and rose up grumbling at the disturbing ways of moderns.

The tall, red ghost of a man burst into the *jacal*, reaching one hand, shaking like a *tule* reed, for the lantern hanging on its nail. The other spread a letter on the table.

"Look at this letter, Perez," cried the man. "Who wrote it?"

"*Ah, Dios!* it is Señor Sandridge," mumbled the old man, approaching. "*Pues, señor,* that letter was written by '*El Chivato*,' as he is called — by the man of Tonia. They say he is a bad man; I do not know. While Tonia slept he wrote the letter and sent it by this old hand of mine to Domingo Sales to be brought to you. Is there anything wrong in the letter? I am very old; and I did not know. *Valgame Dios!* it is a very foolish world; and there is nothing in the house to drink — nothing to drink."

Just then all that Sandridge could think of to do was to go outside and throw himself face downward in the dust by the side of his humming-bird, of whom not a feather fluttered. He was not a *cabellero* by instinct, and he could not understand the niceties of revenge.

A mile away the rider who had ridden past the wagon-shed struck up a harsh, untuneful song, the words of which began:

> Don't you monkey with my Lulu girl
> Or I'll tell you what I'll do ——

THE MARIONETTES

THE policeman was standing at the corner of Twenty-fourth Street and a prodigiously dark alley near where the elevated railroad crosses the street. The time was two o'clock in the morning; the outlook a stretch of cold, drizzling, unsociable blackness until the dawn.

A man, wearing a long overcoat, with his hat tilted down in front, and carrying something in one hand, walked softly but rapidly out of the black alley. The policeman accosted him civilly, but with the assured air that is linked with conscious authority. The hour, the alley's musty reputation, the pedestrian's haste, the burden he carried — these easily combined into the "suspicious circumstances" that required illumination at the officer's hands.

The "suspect" halted readily and tilted back his hat, exposing, in the flicker of the electric lights, an emotionless, smooth countenance with a rather long nose and steady dark eyes. Thrusting his gloved hand into a side pocket of his overcoat, he drew out a card and handed it to the policeman. Holding it to catch the uncertain light, the officer read the name "Charles Spencer James, M.D." The street and number of the address were of a neighborhood so solid and respectable as to subdue even curiosity. The policeman's downward glance at the article carried in the doctor's hand — a handsome medicine case of black leather, with small silver mountings — further endorsed the guarantee of the card.

"All right, doctor," said the officer, stepping aside, with an air of bulky affability. "Orders are to be extra careful. Good many burglars and hold-ups lately. Bad night to be out. Not so cold, but — clammy."

With a formal inclination of his head, and a word or two corroborative of the officer's estimate of the weather, Doctor James continued his somewhat rapid progress. Three times that night had a patrolman accepted his professional card and the sight of his paragon of a medicine case as vouchers for his honesty of person and purpose. Had any one of those officers seen fit, on the morrow, to test the evidence of that card he would have found it borne out by the doctor's name on a handsome doorplate, his presence, calm and well dressed, in his well-equipped office — provided it were not too early, Doctor James being

[*Originally published in* The Black Cat *for April, 1902, The Short Story Publishing Co.*]

a late riser — and the testimony of the neighborhood to his good citizenship, his devotion to his family, and his success as a practitioner the two years he had lived among them.

Therefore, it would have much surprised any one of those zealous guardians of the peace could they have taken a peep into that immaculate medicine case. Upon opening it, the first article to be seen would have been an elegant set of the latest conceived tools used by the "box man," as the ingenious safe burglar now denominates himself. Specially designed and constructed were the implements — the short but powerful "jimmy," the collection of curiously fashioned keys, the blued drills and punches of the finest temper — capable of eating their way into chilled steel as a mouse eats into a cheese, and the clamps that fasten like a leech to the polished door of a safe and pull out the combination knob as a dentist extracts a tooth. In a little pouch in the inner side of the "medicine" case was a four-ounce vial of nitroglycerine, now half empty. Underneath the tools was a mass of crumpled banknotes and a few handfuls of gold coin, the money, altogether, amounting to eight hundred and thirty dollars.

To a very limited circle of friends Doctor James was known as "the Swell 'Greek.' " Half of the mysterious term was a tribute to his cool and gentleman-like manners; the other half denoted, in the argot of the brotherhood, the leader, the planner, the one who, by the power and prestige of his address and position, secured the information upon which they based their plans and desperate enterprises.

Of this elect circle the other members were Skitsie Morgan and Gum Decker, expert "box men," and Leopold Pretzfelder, a jeweller down town, who manipulated the "sparklers" and other ornaments collected by the working trio. All good and loyal men, as loose-tongued as Memnon and as fickle as the North Star.

That night's work had not been considered by the firm to have yielded more than a moderate repayal for their pains. An old-style two-story side-bolt safe in the dingy office of a very wealthy old-style dry-goods firm on a Saturday night should have excreted more than twenty-five hundred dollars. But that was all they found, and they had divided it, the three of them, into equal shares upon the spot, as was their custom. Ten or twelve thousand was what they expected. But one of the proprietors had proved to be just a trifle too old style. Just after dark he had carried home in a shirt box most of the funds on hand.

Doctor James proceeded up Twenty-fourth Street, which was, to all appearance, depopulated. Even the theatrical folk, who affect this district as a place of residence, were long since abed. The drizzle had accumulated upon the street; puddles of it among the stones received the fire of the arc lights, and returned it, shattered into a myriad liquid spangles. A captious wind, shower-soaked and chilling, coughed from the laryngeal flues between the houses.

As the practitioner's foot struck even with the corner of a tall brick residence of more pretension than its fellows the front door popped open, and a bawling Negress clattered down the steps to the pavement. Some medley of words came forth from her mouth, addressed, like as not, to herself.

She looked to be one of that old vassal class of the South — voluble, familiar, loyal, irrepressible; her person pictured it — fat, neat, aproned, kerchiefed.

This sudden apparition, spewed from the silent house, reached the bottom of the steps as Doctor James came opposite. Her brain transferring its energies from sound to sight, she ceased her clamor and fixed her pop-eyes upon the case the doctor carried.

"Bless de Lawd!" was the benison the sight drew from her. "Is you a doctor, suh?"

"Yes, I am a physician," said Doctor James, pausing.

"Den fo' God's sake come and see Mister Chandler, suh. He done had a fit or sump'n. He layin' jist like he wuz dead. Miss Amy sont me to git a doctor. Lawd knows whar old Cindy'd a skeared one up from, if you, suh, hadn't come along. Ef old Mar's knowed one ten-hundredth part of dese doin's dey'd be shootin' gwine on, suh — pistol shootin' — leb'm feet marked off on de ground, and ev'ybody a-duellin'. And dat po' lamb, Miss Amy ——"

"Lead the way," said Doctor James, setting his foot upon the step, "if you want me as a doctor. As an auditor I'm not open for engagements."

The Negress preceded him into the house and up a flight of thickly carpeted stairs. Twice they came to dimly lighted branching hallways. At the second one the now panting conductress turned down a hall, stopping at a door and opening it.

"I done brought de doctor, Miss Amy."

Doctor James entered the room, and bowed slightly to a young lady standing by the side of a bed. He set his medicine case upon a chair, removed his overcoat, throwing it over the case and the back of the chair, and advanced with quiet self-possession to the bedside.

There lay a man, sprawling as he had fallen — a man dressed richly in the prevailing mode, with only his shoes removed; lying relaxed, and as still as the dead.

There emanated from Doctor James an aura of calm force and reserve strength that was as manna in the desert to the weak and desolate among his patrons. Always had women, especially, been attracted by something in his sick-room manner. It was not the indulgent suavity of the fashionable healer, but a manner of poise, of sureness, of ability to overcome fate, of deference and protection and devotion. There was an exploring magnetism in his steadfast, luminous eyes; a latent authority in the impassive, even priestly, tranquillity of his smooth countenance that outwardly fitted him for the part of confidant and consoler. Sometimes, at his first professional visit, women would tell him where they hid their diamonds at night from the burglars.

With the ease of much practice, Doctor James's unroving eyes estimated the order and quality of the room's furnishings. The appointments were rich and costly. The same glance had secured cognizance of the lady's appearance. She was small and scarcely past twenty. Her face possessed the title to a winsome prettiness, now obscured by (you would say) rather a fixed melancholy than the more violent imprint of a sudden sorrow. Upon her forehead, above one eyebrow, was a livid bruise, suffered, the physician's eye told him, within the past six hours. Doctor James's fingers went to the man's wrist. His almost vocal eyes questioned the lady.

"I am Mrs. Chandler," she responded, speaking with the plaintive Southern slur and intonation. "My husband was taken suddenly ill about ten minutes before you came. He has had attacks of heart trouble before — some of them were very bad." His clothed state and the late hour seemed to prompt her to further explanation. "He had been out late; to — a supper, I believe."

Doctor James now turned his attention to his patient. In whichever of his "professions" he happened to be engaged he was wont to honor the "case" or the "job" with his whole interest.

The sick man appeared to be about thirty. His countenance bore a look of boldness and dissipation, but was not without a symmetry of feature and the fine lines drawn by a taste and indulgence in humor that gave the redeeming touch. There was an odor of spilled wine about his clothes.

The physician laid back his outer garments, and then, with a penknife, slit the shirt-front from collar to waist. The obstacles cleared, he laid his ear to the heart and listened intently.

"Mitral regurgitation?" he said, softly, when he rose. The words ended with the rising inflection of uncertainty. Again he listened long; and this time he said, "Mitral insufficiency," with the accent of an assured diagnosis.

"Madam," he began, in the reassuring tones that he had so often allayed anxiety, "there is a probability ——" As he slowly turned his head to face the lady, he saw her fall, white and swooning, into the arms of the old Negress.

"Po' lamb! Po' lamb! Has dey done killed Aunt Cindy's own blessed child? May de Lawd 'stroy wid his wrath dem what stole her away; what break dat angel heart; what left ——"

"Lift her feet," said Doctor James, assisting to support the drooping form. "Where is her room? She must be put to bed."

"In here, suh." The woman nodded her kerchiefed head toward a door. "Dat's Miss Amy's room."

They carried her in there, and laid her on the bed. Her pulse was faint, but regular. She passed from the swoon, without recovering consciousness, into a profound slumber.

"She is quite exhausted," said the physician. "Sleep is a good remedy. When she wakes, give her a toddy — with an egg in it, if she can take it. How did she get that bruise upon her forehead?"

"She done got a lick there, suh. De po' lamb fell —— No, suh" — the old woman's racial mutability swept her in a sudden flare of indignation — "old Cindy ain't gwineter lie for dat debble. He done it, suh. May de Lawd wither de hand what — dar now! Cindy promise her sweet lamb she ain't gwine tell. Miss Amy got hurt, suh, on de head."

Doctor James stepped to a stand where a handsome lamp burned, and turned the flame low.

"Stay here with your mistress," he ordered, "and keep quiet so she will sleep. If she wakes, give her the toddy. If she grows any weaker, let me know. There is something strange about it."

"Dar's mo' strange t'ings dan dat 'round here," began the Negress, but the physician hushed her in a seldom-employed peremptory, concentrated voice with which he had often allayed hysteria itself. He returned to the other room, closing the door softly behind him. The man on the bed had not moved, but his eyes were open. His lips seemed to form words. Doctor James bent his head to listen. "The money! the money!" was what they were whispering.

"Can you understand what I say?" asked the doctor, speaking low, but distinctly.

The head nodded slightly.

"I am a physician, sent for by your wife. You are Mr. Chandler, I am told. You are quite ill. You must not excite or distress yourself at all."

The patient's eyes seemed to beckon to him. The doctor stooped to catch the same faint words.

"The money — the twenty thousand dollars."

"Where is this money? — in the bank?"

The eyes expressed a negative. "Tell her" — the whisper was growing fainter — "the twenty thousand dollars — her money" — his eyes wandered about the room.

"You have placed this money somewhere?" — Doctor James's voice was toiling like a siren's to conjure the secret from the man's failing intelligence — "Is it in this room?"

He thought he saw a fluttering assent in the dimming eyes. The pulse under his fingers was as fine and small as a silk thread.

There arose in Doctor James's brain and heart the instincts of his other profession. Promptly, as he acted in everything, he decided to learn the whereabouts of this money, and at the calculated and certain cost of a human life.

Drawing from his pocket a little pad of prescription blanks, he scribbled upon one of them a formula suited, according to the best practice, to the needs of the sufferer. Going to the door of the inner room, he softly called the old woman, gave her the prescription, and bade her take it to some drug store and fetch the medicine.

When she had gone, muttering to herself, the doctor stepped to the bedside of the lady. She still slept soundly; her pulse was a little stronger; her forehead was cool, save where the inflammation of the bruise extended, and a slight moisture covered it. Unless disturbed, she would yet sleep for hours. He found the key in the door, and locked it after him when he returned.

Doctor James looked at his watch. He could call half an hour his own, since before that time the old woman could scarcely return from her mission. Then he sought and found water in a pitcher and a glass tumbler. Opening his medicine case he took out the vial containing the nitroglycerine — "the oil," as his brethren of the brace-and-bit term it.

One drop of the faint yellow, thickish liquid he let fall in the tumbler. He took out his silver hypodermic syringe case, and screwed the needle into its place. Carefully measuring each modicum of water in the graduated glass barrel of the syringe, he diluted the one drop with nearly half a tumbler of water.

Two hours earlier that night Doctor James had, with that syringe, injected the undiluted liquid into a hole drilled in the lock of a safe, and had destroyed, with one dull explosion, the machinery that controlled the movement of the bolts. He now purposed, with the same means, to shiver the prime machinery of a human being — to rend its heart — and each shock was for the sake of the money to follow.

The same means, but in a different guise. Whereas, that was the giant in its rude, primary dynamic strength, this was the courtier, whose no less deadly arms were concealed by velvet and lace. For the liquid in the tumbler and in the syringe that the physician carefully filled was now a solution of glonoin, the most powerful heart stimulant known to medical science. Two ounces had riven the solid door of the iron safe; with one fiftieth part of a minim he was now about to still forever the intricate mechanism of a human life.

But not immediately. It was not so intended. First there would be a quick increase of vitality; a powerful impetus given to every organ and faculty. The heart would respond bravely to the fatal spur; the blood in the veins return more rapidly to its source.

But, as Doctor James well knew, over-stimulation in this form of heart disease means death, as sure as by a rifle shot. When the clogged arteries should suffer congestion from the increased flow of blood, pumped into them by the power of the burglar's "oil," they would rapidly become "no thoroughfare," and the fountain of life would cease to flow.

The physician bared the chest of the unconscious Chandler. Easily and skilfully he injected, subcutaneously, the contents of the syringe into the muscles of the region over the heart. True to his neat habits in both professions, he next carefully dried his needle and re-inserted the fine wire that threaded it when not in use.

In three minutes Chandler opened his eyes, and spoke, in a voice faint but audible, inquiring who attended upon him. Doctor James again explained his presence there.

"Where is my wife?" asked the patient.

"She is asleep — from exhaustion and worry," said the doctor. "I would not awaken her, unless ——"

"It isn't — necessary." Chandler spoke with spaces between his words caused by his short breath that some demon was driving too fast. "She wouldn't — thank you to disturb her — on my — account."

Doctor James drew a chair to the bedside. Conversation must not be squandered.

"A few minutes ago," he began, in the grave, candid tones of his other profession, "you were trying to tell me something regarding some money. I do not seek your confidence, but it is my duty to advise you that anxiety and worry will work against your recovery. If you have any communication to make about this — to relieve your mind about this — twenty thousand dollars, I think was the amount you mentioned — you would better do so."

Chandler could not turn his head, but he rolled his eyes in the direction of the speaker. "Did I — say where this — money is?"

"No," answered the physician. "I only inferred, from your scarcely intelligible words, that you felt a solicitude concerning its safety. If it is in this room ——"

Doctor James paused. Did he only seem to perceive a flicker of understanding, a gleam of suspicion upon the ironical features of his patient? Had he seemed too eager? Had he said too much? Chandler's next words restored his confidence.

"Where — should it be," he gasped, "but in — the safe — there?"

With his eyes he indicated a corner of the room, where now, for the first time, the doctor perceived a small iron safe, half-concealed by the trailing end of a window curtain.

Rising, he took the sick man's wrist. His pulse was beating in great throbs, with ominous intervals between.

"Lift your arm," said Doctor James.

"You know — I can't move, Doctor."

The physician stepped swiftly to the hall door, opened it, and listened. All was still. Without further circumvention he went to the safe, and examined it. Of a primitive make and simple design, it afforded a little more security than protection against light-fingered servants. To his skill it was a mere toy, a thing of straw and pasteboard. The money was as good as in his hands. With his clamps he could draw the knob, punch the tumblers, and open the door in two minutes. Perhaps, in another way, he might open it in one.

Kneeling upon the floor, he laid his ear to the combination plate, and slowly turned the knob. As he had surmised, it was locked at only a "day com." — upon one number. His keen ear caught the faint warning click as the tumbler was disturbed; he used the clue — the handle turned. He swung the door wide open.

The interior of the safe was bare — not even a scrap of paper rested within the hollow iron cube.

Doctor James rose to his feet and walked back to the bed.

A thick dew had formed upon the dying man's brow, but there was a mocking, grim smile on his lips and in his eyes.

"I never — saw it before," he said, painfully, "medicine and — burglary wedded! Do you — make the — combination pay — dear Doctor?"

Than that situation afforded, there was never a more rigorous test of Doctor James's greatness. Trapped by the diabolic humor of his victim into a position both ridiculous and unsafe, he maintained his dignity as well as his presence of mind. Taking out his watch, he waited for the man to die.

"You were — just a shade — too — anxious — about that money. But it never was — in any danger — from you, dear Doctor. It's safe. Perfectly safe. It's all — in the hands — of the bookmakers. Twenty — thousand — Amy's money. I played it at the races — lost every — cent of it. I've been a pretty bad boy, Burglar — excuse me — Doctor, but I've been a square sport. I don't think — I ever met — such an — eighteen-carat rascal as you are, Doctor — excuse me — Burglar, in all my rounds. Is it contrary — to the ethics — of your — gang, Burglar, to give a victim — excuse me — patient, a drink of water?"

Doctor James brought him a drink. He could scarcely swallow it. The reaction from the powerful drug was coming in regular, intensifying waves. But his moribund fancy must have one more grating fling.

"Gambler — drunkard — spendthrift — I've been those, but — a doctor-burglar!"

The physician indulged himself to but one reply to the other's caustic taunts. Bending low to catch Chandler's fast crystallizing gaze, he pointed to the sleeping lady's door with a gesture so stern and significant that the prostrate man half-lifted his head, with his remaining strength, to see. He saw nothing; but he caught the cold words of the doctor — the last sounds he was to hear:

"I never yet — struck a woman."

It were vain to attempt to con such men. There is no curriculum that can reckon with them in its ken. They are offshoots from the types whereof men say, "He will do this," or "He will do that." We only know that they exist; and that we can observe them, and tell one another of their bare performances, as children watch and speak of the marionettes.

Yet it were a droll study in egoism to consider these two — one an assassin and a robber, standing above his victim; the other baser in his offences, if a lesser law-breaker, lying, abhorred, in the house of the wife he had persecuted, spoiled, and smitten, one a tiger, the other a dog-wolf — to consider each of them sickening at the foulness of the other; and each flourishing out of the mire of his manifest guilt his own immaculate standard — of conduct, if not of honor.

The one retort of Doctor James must have struck home to the other's remaining shreds of shame and manhood, for it proved the *coup de grâce*. A deep blush suffused his face — an ignominious *rosa mortis;* the respiration ceased, and, with scarcely a tremor, Chandler expired. Close following upon his last breath came the Negress, bringing the medicine. With a hand gently pressing upon the closed eyelids, Doctor James told her of the end. Not grief, but a hereditary *rapprochement* with death in the abstract, moved her to a dismal, watery sniffling, accompanied by her usual jeremiad.

"Dar now! It's in de Lawd's hands. He am de jedge ob de transgressor, and de suppo't of dem in distress. He gwine hab suppo't us now. Cindy done paid out de last quarter fer dis bottle of physic."

"Do I understand," asked Doctor James, "that Mrs. Chandler has no money?"

"Money, suh? You know what make Miss Amy fall down and so weak? Stahvation, suh. Nothin' to eat in dis house but some crumbly crackers in three days. Dat angel sell her finger rings and watch mont's ago. Dis fine house, suh, wid de red cyarpets and shiny bureaus, it's all hired; and de man talkin' scan'lous about de rent. Dat debble — 'scuse me, Lawd — he done in Yo' hands fer jedgment, now — he made way wid everything."

The physician's silence encouraged her to continue. The history that he gleaned from Cindy's disordered monologue was an old one, of illusion, wilfulness, disaster, cruelty, and pride. Standing out from the blurred panorama of her gabble were little clear pictures — an ideal home in the far South; a quickly repented marriage; an unhappy season, full of wrongs and abuse, and, of late, an inheritance of money that promised deliverance; its seizure and waste by the dog-wolf during a two months' absence, and his return in the midst of a scandalous carouse. Unobtruded, but visible between every line, ran a pure white thread through the smudged warp of the story — the simple all-enduring sublime love of the old Negress, following her mistress unswervingly through everything to the end.

When at last she paused, the physician spoke, asking if the house contained whiskey or liquor of any sort. There was, the old woman informed him, half a bottle of brandy left in the sideboard by the dog-wolf.

"Prepare a toddy as I told you," said Doctor James. "Wake your mistress; have her drink it, and tell her what has happened."

Some ten minutes afterward, Mrs. Chandler entered, supported by old Cindy's arm. She appeared to be a little stronger since her sleep and the stimulant she had taken. Doctor James had covered, with a sheet, the form upon the bed.

The lady turned her mournful eyes once, with a half-frightened look, toward it, and pressed closer to her protector. Her eyes were dry and bright. Sorrow seemed to have done its utmost with her. The fount of tears was dried; feeling itself paralyzed.

Doctor James was standing near the table, his overcoat donned, his hat and medicine case in his hand. His face was calm and impassive — practice had inured him to the sight of human suffering. His lambent brown eyes alone expressed a discreet professional sympathy.

He spoke kindly and briefly, stating that, as the hour was late, and assistance, no doubt, difficult to procure, he would himself send the proper persons to attend to the necessary finalities.

"One matter, in conclusion," said the doctor, pointing to the safe with its still wide-open door. "Your husband, Mrs. Chandler, toward the end, felt that he could not live; and directed me to open that safe, giving me the number upon which the combination is set. In case you may need to use it, you will remember that the number is forty-one. Turn several times to the right; then to the left once; stop at forty-one. He would not permit me to waken you, though he knew the end was near.

"In that safe he said he had placed a sum of money not large — but enough to enable you to carry out his last request. That was that you should return to your old home, and, in after days, when time shall have made it easier, forgive his many sins against you."

He pointed to the table, where lay an orderly pile of banknotes, surmounted by two stacks of gold coins.

"The money is there — as he described it — eight hundred and thirty dollars. I beg to leave my card with you, in case I can be of any service later on."

So, he had thought of her — and kindly — at the last! So late! And yet the lie fanned into life one last spark of tenderness where she had thought all was turned to ashes and dust. She cried aloud "Rob! Rob!" She turned, and, upon the ready bosom of her true servitor, diluted her grief in relieving tears. It is well to think, also, that in the years to follow, the murderer's falsehood shone like a little star above the grave of love, comforting her, and gaining the forgiveness that is good in itself, whether asked for or no.

Hushed and soothed upon the dark bosom, like a child, by a crooning, babbling sympathy, at last she raised her head — but the doctor was gone.

THE MAN HIGHER UP

Across our two dishes of spaghetti, in a corner of Provenzano's restaurant, Jeff Peters was explaining to me the three kinds of graft.

Every winter Jeff comes to New York to eat spaghetti, to watch the shipping in East River from the depths of his chinchilla overcoat, and to lay in a supply of Chicago-made clothing at one of the Fulton Street stores. During the other three seasons he may be found further west — his range is from Spokane to Tampa. In his profession he takes a pride which he supports and defends with a serious and unique philosophy of ethics. His profession is no new one. He is an incorporated, uncapitalized, unlimited asylum for the reception of the restless and unwise dollars of his fellow men.

In the wilderness of stone in which Jeff seeks his annual lonely holiday he is glad to palaver of his many adventures, as a boy will whistle after sundown in a wood. Wherefore, I mark on my calendar the time of his coming, and open a question of privilege at Provenzano's concerning the little wine-stained table in the corner between the rakish rubber plant and the framed palazzio della something on the wall.

"There are two kinds of grafts," said Jeff, "that ought to be wiped out by law. I mean Wall Street speculation, and burglary."

"Nearly everybody will agree with you as to one of them," said I, with a laugh.

"Well, burglary ought to be wiped out, too," said Jeff; and I wondered whether the laugh had been redundant.

"About three months ago," said Jeff, "it was my privilege to become familiar with a sample of each of the aforesaid branches of illegitimate art. I was *sine qua grata* with a member of the housebreakers' union and one of the John D. Napoleons of finance at the same time."

"Interesting combination," said I, with a yawn. "Did I tell you I bagged a duck and a ground squirrel at one shot last week over in the Ramapos?" I knew well how to draw Jeff's stories.

"Let me tell you first about these barnacles that clog the wheels of society by poisoning the springs of rectitude with their upas-like eye," said Jeff, with the pure gleam of the muck-raker in his own.

"As I said, three months ago I got into bad company. There are two times in a man's life when he does this — when he's dead broke, and when he's rich.

"Now and then the most legitimate business runs out of luck. It

113

was out in Arkansas I made the wrong turn at a cross-road, and drives into this town of Peavine by mistake. It seems I had already assaulted and disfigured Peavine the spring of the year before. I had sold $600 worth of young fruit trees there — plums, cherries, peaches and pears. The Peaviners were keeping an eye on the country road and hoping I might pass that way again. I drove down Main Street as far as the Crystal Palace drug-store before I realized I had committed ambush upon myself and my white horse Bill.

"The Peaviners took me by surprise and Bill by the bridle and began a conversation that wasn't entirely disassociated with the subject of fruit trees. A committee of 'em ran some trace-chains through the armholes of my vest and escorted me through their gardens and orchards.

"Their fruit trees hadn't lived up to their labels. Most of 'em had turned out to be persimmons and dogwoods, with a grove or two of blackjacks and poplars. The only one that showed any signs of bearing anything was a fine young cottonwood that had put forth a hornet's nest and half of an old corset-cover.

"The Peaviners protracted our fruitless stroll to the edge of town. They took my watch and money on account; and they kept Bill and the wagon as hostages. They said the first time one of them dogwood trees put forth Amsden's June peach I might come back and get my things. Then they took off the trace-chains and jerked their thumbs in the direction of the Rocky Mountains; and I struck a Lewis and Clark lope for the swollen rivers and impenetrable forests.

"When I regained intellectualness I found myself walking into an unidentified town on the A., T. & S. F. railroad. The Peaviners hadn't left anything in my pockets except a plug of chewing — they wasn't after my life — and saved it. I bit off a chunk and sits down on a pile of ties by the track to recogitate my sensations of thought and perspicacity.

"And then along comes a fast freight which slows up a little at the town; and off of it drops a black bundle that rolls for twenty yards in a cloud of dust and then gets up and begins to spit soft coal and interjections. I see it is a young man broad across the face, dressed more for Pullmans than freights, and with a cheerful kind of smile in spite of it all that made Phœbe Snow's job look like a chimney-sweep's.

" 'Fall off?' says I.

" 'Nunk,' says he. 'Got off. Arrived at my destination. What town is this?'

" 'Haven't looked it up on the map yet,' says I. 'I got in about five minutes before you did. How does it strike you?'

" 'Hard,' says he, twisting one of his arms around. 'I believe that shoulder — no, it's all right.'

"He stoops over to brush the dust off his clothes, when out of his pocket drops a fine, nine-inch burglar's steel jimmy. He picks it up and looks at me sharp, and then grins and holds out his hand.

" 'Brother,' says he, 'greetings. Didn't I see you in Southern Missouri last summer selling colored sand at half-a-dollar a teaspoonful to put into lamps to keep the oil from exploding?'

" 'Oil,' says I, 'never explodes. It's the gas that forms that explodes.' But I shakes hands with him, anyway.

" 'My name's Bill Bassett,' says he to me, 'and if you'll call it professional pride instead of conceit, I'll inform you that you have the pleasure of meeting the best burglar that ever set a gum-shoe on ground drained by the Mississippi River.'

"Well, me and this Bill Bassett sits on the ties and exchanges brags as artists in kindred lines will do. It seems he didn't have a cent, either, and we went into close caucus. He explained why an able burglar sometimes had to travel on freights by telling me that a servant girl had played him false in Little Rock, and he was making a quick getaway.

" 'It's part of my business,' says Bill Bassett, 'to play up to the ruffles when I want to make a riffle as Raffles. 'Tis loves that makes the bit go 'round. Show me a house with the swag in it and a pretty parlor-maid, and you might as well call the silver melted down and sold, and me spilling truffles and that Château stuff on the napkin under my chin, while the police are calling it an inside job just because the old lady's nephew teaches a Bible class. I first make an impression on the girl,' says Bill, 'and when she lets me inside I make an impression on the locks. But this one in Little Rock done me,' says he. 'She saw me taking a trolley ride with another girl, and when I came 'round on the night she was to leave the door open for me it was fast. And I had keys made for the doors upstairs. But, no sir. She had sure cut off my locks. She was a Delilah,' says Bill Bassett.

"It seems that Bill tried to break in anyhow with his jimmy, but the girl emitted a succession of bravura noises like the top-riders of a tally-ho, and Bill had to take all the hurdles between there and the depot. As he had no baggage they tried hard to check his departure, but he made a train that was just pulling out.

" 'Well,' says Bill Bassett, when we had exchanged memoirs of our dead lives, 'I could eat. This town don't look like it was kept under a

Yale lock. Suppose we commit some mild atrocity that will bring in temporary expense money. I don't suppose you've brought along any hair tonic or rolled gold watch-chains, or similar law-defying swindles that you could sell on the plaza to the pikers of the paretic populace, have you?'

" 'No,' says I, 'I left an elegant line of Patagonia diamond earrings and rainy-day sunbursts in my valise at Peavine. But they're to stay there till some of them black-gum trees begin to glut the market with yellow clings and Japanese plums. I reckon we can't count on them unless we take Luther Burbank in for a partner.'

" 'Very well,' says Bassett, 'we'll do the best we can. Maybe after dark I'll borrow a hairpin from some lady, and open the Farmers and Drovers Marine Bank with it.'

"While we were talking, up pulls a passenger train to the depot near by. A person in a high hat gets off on the wrong side of the train and comes tripping down the track towards us. He was a little, fat man with a big nose and rat's eyes, but dressed expensive, and carrying a hand-satchel careful, as if it had eggs or railroad bonds in it. He passes by us and keeps on down the track, not appearing to notice the town.

" 'Come on,' says Bill Bassett to me, starting after him.

" 'Where?' I asks.

" 'Lordy!' says Bill, 'had you forgot you was in the desert? Didn't you see Colonel Manna drop down right before your eyes? Don't you hear the rustling of General Raven's wings? I'm surprised at you, Elijah.'

"We overtook the stranger in the edge of some woods, and, as it was after sun-down and in a quiet place, nobody saw us stop him. Bill takes the silk hat off the man's head and brushes it with his sleeve and puts it back.

" 'What does this mean, sir?' says the man.

" 'When I wore one of these,' says Bill, 'and felt embarrassed, I always done that. Not having one now I had to use yours. I hardly know how to begin, sir, in explaining our business with you, but I guess we'll try your pockets first.'

"Bill Bassett felt in all of them, and looked disgusted.

" 'Not even a watch,' he says. 'Ain't you ashamed of yourself, you whited sculpture? Going about dressed like a head-waiter, and financed like a Count. You haven't even got carfare. What did you do with your transfer?'

"The man speaks up and says he has no assets or valuables of any sort. But Bassett takes his hand-satchel and opens it. Out comes some collars and socks and a half a page of a newspaper clipped out. Bill reads the clipping careful, and holds out his hand to the held-up party.

" 'Brother,' says he, 'greetings! Accept the apologies of friends. I am Bill Bassett, the burglar. Mr. Peters, you must make the acquaintance of Mr. Alfred E. Ricks. Shake hands. Mr. Peters,' says Bill, 'stands about halfway between me and you, Mr. Ricks, in the line of havoc and corruption. He always gives something for the money he gets. I'm glad to meet you, Mr. Ricks — you and Mr. Peters. This is the first time I ever attended a full gathering of the National Synod of Sharks—housebreaking, swindling, and financiering all represented. Please examine Mr. Rick's credentials, Mr. Peters.'

"The piece of newspaper that Bill Bassett handed me had a good picture of this Ricks on it. It was a Chicago paper, and it had obloquies of Ricks in every paragraph. By reading it over I harvested the intelligence that said alleged Ricks had laid off all that portion of the State of Florida that lies under water into town lots and sold 'em to alleged innocent investors from his magnificently furnished offices in Chicago. After he had taken in a hundred thousand or so dollars one of these fussy purchasers that are always making trouble (I've had 'em actually try gold watches I've sold 'em with acid) took a cheap excursion down to the land where it is always just before supper to look at his lot and see if it didn't need a new paling or two on the fence, and market a few lemons in time for the Christmas present trade. He hires a surveyor to find his lot for him. They run the line out and find the flourishing town of Paradise Hollow, so advertised, to be about 40 rods and 16 poles S., 27° E. of the middle of Lake Okeeshobee. This man's lot was under thirty-six feet of water, and, besides, had been preëmpted so long by the alligators and gars that his title looked fishy.

"Naturally, the man goes back to Chicago and makes it as hot for Alfred E. Ricks as the morning after a prediction of snow by the weather bureau. Ricks defied the allegation, but he couldn't deny the alligators. One morning the papers came out with a column about it, and Ricks come out by the fire-escape. It seems the alleged authorities had beat him to the safe-deposit box where he kept his winnings, and Ricks has to westward ho! with only feetwear and a dozen 15½ English pokes in his shopping bag. He happened to have some mileage left in his book, and that took him as far as the town in the wilderness where he was spilled out on me and Bill Bassett as Elijah III with not a raven in sight for any of us.

"Then this Alfred E. Ricks lets out a squeak that he is hungry, too, and denies the hypothesis that he is good for the value, let alone the price, of a meal. And so, there was the three of us, representing, if we had a mind to draw syllogisms and parabolas, labor and trade and capital. Now, when trade has no capital there isn't a dicker to be made. And when capital has no money there's a stagnation in steak and onions. That put it up to the man with the jimmy.

" 'Brother bushrangers,' says Bill Bassett, 'never yet, in trouble, did I desert a pal. Hard by, in yon wood, I seem to see unfurnished lodgings. Let us go there and wait till dark.'

"There was an old deserted cabin in the grove, and we took possession of it. After dark Bill Bassett tells us to wait, and goes out for half an hour. He comes back with a armful of bread and spareribs and pies.

" 'Panhandled 'em at a farmhouse on Washita Avenue,' says he. 'Eat, drink, and be leary.'

"The full moon was coming up bright, so we sat on the floor of the cabin and ate in the light of it. And this Bill Bassett begins to brag.

" 'Sometimes,' says he, with his mouth full of country produce, 'I lose all patience with you people that think you are higher up in the profession than I am. Now, what could either of you have done in the present emergency to set us on our feet again? Could you do it, Ricksy?"

" 'I must confess, Mr. Bassett,' says Ricks, speaking near inaudible out of a slice of pie, 'that at this immediate juncture I could not, perhaps, promote an enterprise to relieve the situation. Large operations, such as I direct, naturally require careful preparation in advance. I —'

" 'I know, Ricksy,' breaks in Bill Bassett. 'You needn't finish. You need $500 to make the first payment on a blond typewriter, and four roomsful of quartered oak furniture. And you need $500 more for advertising contracts. And you need two weeks' time for the fish to begin to bite. Your line of relief would be about as useful in an emergency as advocating municipal ownership to cure a man suffocated by eighty-cent gas. And your graft ain't much swifter, Brother Peters,' he winds up.

" 'Oh,' says I, 'I haven't seen you turn anything into gold with your wand yet, Mr. Good Fairy. Most anybody could rub the magic ring for a little left-over victuals.'

" 'That was only getting the pumpkin ready,' says Bassett, braggy and cheerful. 'The coach and six'll drive up to the door before you know it, Miss Cinderella. Maybe you've got some scheme under your sleeve-holders that will give us a start.'

" 'Son,' says I, 'I'm fifteen years older than you are, and young enough yet to take out an endowment policy. I've been broke before.

We can see the lights of that town not half a mile away. I learned under Montague Silver, the greatest street man that ever spoke from a wagon. There are hundreds of men walking those streets this moment with grease spots on their clothes. Give me a gasoline lamp, a dry-goods box, and a two-dollar bar of white castile soap, cut into little ——'

" 'Where's your two dollars?' snickered Bill Bassett into my discourse. There was no use arguing with that burglar.

" 'No,' he goes on; 'you're both babes-in-the-wood. Finance has closed the mahogany desk, and trade has put the shutters up. Both of you look to labor to start the wheels going. All right. You admit it. To-night I'll show you what Bill Bassett can do.'

"Bassett tells me and Ricks not to leave the cabin till he comes back, even if it's daylight, and then he starts off toward town, whistling gay.

"This Alfred E. Ricks pulls off his shoes and his coat, lays a silk handkerchief over his hat, and lays down on the floor.

" 'I think I will endeavor to secure a little slumber,' he squeaks. 'The day has been fatiguing. Good-night, my dear Mr. Peters.'

" 'My regards to Morpheus,' says I. 'I think I'll sit up a while.'

"About two o'clock, as near as I could guess by my watch in Peavine, home comes our laboring man and kicks up Ricks, and calls us to the streak of bright moonlight shining in the cabin door. Then he spreads out five packages of one thousand dollars each on the floor, and begins to cackle over the nest-egg like a hen.

" 'I'll tell you a few things about that town,' says he. 'It's named Rocky Springs, and they're building a Masonic temple, and it looks like the Democratic candidate for mayor is going to get soaked by a Pop, and Judge Tucker's wife, who has been down with pleurisy, is some better. I had a talk on these liliputian thesises before I could get a siphon in the fountain of knowledge that I was after. And there's a bank there called the Lumberman's Fidelity and Plowman's Savings Institution. It closed for business yesterday with $23,000 cash on hand. It will open this morning with $18,000 — all silver — that's the reason I didn't bring more. There you are, trade and capital. Now, will you be bad?"

" 'My young friend,' says Alfred E. Ricks, holding up his hands, 'have you robbed this bank? Dear me, dear me!'

" 'You couldn't call it that,' says Bassett. ' "Robbing" sounds harsh. All I had to do was to find out what street it was on. That town is so quiet that I could stand on the corner and hear the tumblers clicking in that safe lock — "right to 45; left twice to 80; right once to 60; left to 15" — as plain as the Yale captain giving orders in the football dialect. Now, boys,' says Bassett, 'this is an early rising town. They tell me the citizens are all up and stirring before daylight. I asked what for, and they said because breakfast was ready at that time. And what of merry Robin Hood? It must be Yoicks! and away with the tinkers' chorus. I'll stake you. How much do you want? Speak up. Capital.'

" 'My dear young friend,' says this ground squirrel of a Ricks, standing on his hind legs and juggling nuts in his paws, 'I have friends in Denver who would assist me. If I had a hundred dollars I ——'

"Bassett unpins a package of the currency and throws five twenties to Ricks.

" 'Trade, how much?' he says to me.

" 'Put your money up, Labor,' says I. 'I never yet drew upon honest toil for its hard-earned pittance. The dollars I get are surplus ones that are burning the pockets of damfools and greenhorns. When I stand on a street corner and sell a solid gold diamond ring to a yap for $3.00, I make just $2.60. And I know he's going to give it to a girl in return for all the benefits accruing from a $125.00 ring. His profits are $122.00. Which of us is the biggest fakir?'

" 'And when you sell a poor woman a pinch of sand for fifty cents to keep her lamp from exploding,' says Bassett, 'what do you figure her gross earnings to be, with sand at forty cents a ton?'

" 'Listen,' says I. 'I instruct her to keep her lamp clean and well filled. If she does that it can't burst. And with the sand in it she knows it can't and she don't worry. It's a kind of Industrial Christian Science. She pays fifty cents, and gets both Rockefeller and Mrs. Eddy on the job. It ain't everybody that can let the gold-dust twins do their work.'

"Alfred E. Ricks all but licks the dust off of Bill Bassett's shoes.

" 'My dear young friend,' says he, 'I will never forget your generosity. Heaven will reward you. But let me implore you to turn from your ways of violence and crime.'

" 'Mousie,' says Bill, 'the hole in the wainscoting for yours. Your dogmas and inculcations sound to me like the last words of a bicycle pump. What has your high moral, elevator-service system of pillage brought you to? Penuriousness and want. Even Brother Peters, who insists upon contaminating the art of robbery with theories of commerce and trade, admitted he was on the lift. Both of you live by the gilded rule. Brother Peters,' says Bill, 'you'd better choose a slice of this embalmed currency. You're welcome.'

"I told Bill Bassett once more to put his money in his pocket. I never had the respect for burglary that some people have. I always gave something for the money I took, even if it was only some little trifle of a souvenir to remind 'em not to get caught again.

"And then Alfred E. Ricks grovels at Bill's feet again, and bids us adieu. He says he will have a team at a farmhouse, and drive to the station below, and take the train for Denver. It salubrified the atmosphere when that lamentable bollworm took his departure. He was a disgrace to every non-industrial profession in the country. With all his big schemes and fine offices he had wound up unable even to get an honest meal except by the kindness of a strange and maybe unscrupulous burglar. I was glad to see him go, though I felt a little sorry for him, now that he was ruined forever. What could such a man do without a big capital to work with? Why, Alfred E. Ricks, as we left him, was as helpless as a turtle on its back. He couldn't have worked a scheme to beat a little girl out of a penny slate-pencil.

"When me and Bill Bassett was left alone I did a little sleight-of-mind turn in my head with a trade secret at the end of it. Thinks I, I'll show this Mr. Burglar Man the difference between business and labor. He had hurt some of my professional self-adulation by casting his Persians upon commerce and trade.

" 'I won't take any of your money as a gift, Mr. Bassett,' says I to him, 'but if you'll pay my expenses as a travelling companion until we get out of the danger zone of the immoral deficit you have caused in this town's finances to-night I'll be obliged.'

"Bill Bassett agreed to that, and we hiked westward as soon as we could catch a safe train.

"When we got to a town in Arizona called Los Perros I suggested that we once more try our luck on terra-cotta. That was the home of Montague Silver, my old instructor, now retired from business. I knew Monty would stake me to web money if I could show him a fly buzzing 'round in the locality. Bill Bassett said all towns looked alike to him as he worked mainly in the dark. So we got off the train in Los Perros, a fine little town in the silver region.

"I had an elegant little sure thing in the way of a commercial sling-shot that I intended to hit Bassett behind the ear with. I wasn't going to take his money while he was asleep, but I was going to leave him with a lottery ticket that would represent in experience to him $4,755 — I think that was the amount he had when we got off the train. But the first time I hinted to him about an investment, he turns on me and disencumbers himself of the following terms and expressions.

" 'Brother Peters,' says he, 'it ain't a bad idea to go into an enterprise of some kind, as you suggest. I think I will. But if I do it will be such a cold proposition that nobody but Robert E. Peary and Charlie

Fairbanks will be able to sit on the board of directors.'

" 'I thought you might want to turn your money over,' says I.

" 'I do, says he, 'frequently. I can't sleep on one side all night. I'll tell you, Brother Peters,' says he, 'I'm going to start a poker room. I don't seem to care for the humdrum of swindling, such as peddling egg-beaters and working off breakfast food on Barnum and Bailey for sawdust to strew in their circus rings. But the gambling business,' says he, 'from the profitable side of the table is a good compromise between swiping silver spoons and selling penwipers at a Waldorf-Astoria charity bazar.'

" 'Then,' says I, 'Mr. Bassett, you don't care to talk over my little business proposition?'

" 'Why,' says he, 'do you know, you can't get a Pasteur institute to start up within fifty miles of where I live. I bite so seldom.'

"So, Bassett rents a room over a saloon and looks around for some furniture and chromos. The same night I went to Monty Silver's house, and he let me have $200 on my prospects. Then I went to the only store in Los Perros that sold playing cards and bought every deck in the house. The next morning when the store opened I was there bringing all the cards back with me. I said that my partner that was going to back me in the game had changed his mind; and I wanted to sell the cards back again. The storekeeper took 'em at half price.

"Yes, I was seventy-five dollars loser up to that time. But while I had the cards that night I marked every one in every deck. That was labor. And then trade and commerce had their innings, and the bread I had cast upon the waters began to come back in the form of cottage pudding with wine sauce.

"Of course I was among the first to buy chips at Bill Bassett's game. He had bought the only cards there was to be had in town; and I knew the back of every one of them better than I know the back of my head when the barber shows me my haircut in the two mirrors.

"When the game closed I had the five thousand and a few odd dollars, and all Bill Bassett had was the wanderlust and a black cat he had bought for a mascot. Bill shook hands with me when I left.

" 'Brother Peters,' says he, 'I have no business being in business. I was preordained to labor. When a No. 1 burglar tries to make a James out of his jimmy he perpetrates an improfundity. You have a well-oiled and efficacious system of luck at cards,' says he. 'Peace go with you.' And I never afterward sees Bill Bassett again."

"Well, Jeff," said I, when the Autolycan adventurer seemed to have divulged the gist of his tale, "I hope you took care of the money.

That would be a respecta — that is a considerable working capital if you should choose some day to settle down to some sort of regular business."

"Me?" said Jeff, virtuously. "You can bet I've taken care of that five thousand."

He tapped his coat over the region of his chest exultantly.

"Gold mining stock," he explained, "every cent of it. Shares par value one dollar. Bound to go up 500 per cent. within a year. Non-assessable. The Blue Gopher Mine. Just discovered a month ago. Better get in yourself if you've any spare dollars on hand."

"Sometimes," said I, "these mines are not ——"

"Oh, this one's solid as an old goose," said Jeff. "Fifty thousand dollars' worth of ore in sight, and 10 per cent. monthly earnings guaranteed."

He drew a long envelope from his pocket and cast it on the table.

"Always carry it with me," said he. "So the burglar can't corrupt or the capitalist break in and water it."

I looked at the beautifully engraved certificate of stock.

"In Colorado, I see," said I. "And, by the way, Jeff, what was the name of the little man who went to Denver — the one you and Bill met at the station?"

"Alfred E. Ricks," said Jeff, "was the toad's designation."

"I see," said I, "the president of this mining company signs himself A. L. Fredericks. I was wondering —"

"Let me see that stock," said Jeff quickly, almost snatching it from me.

To mitigate, even though slightly, the embarrassment I summoned the waiter and ordered another bottle of the Barbera. I thought it was the least I could do.

www.ingramcontent.com/pod-product-compliance
Lightning Source LLC
Chambersburg PA
CBHW020658180626
46816CB00003B/1339